Mom Wife Witch

Mom Wife Witch

ISBM-13: 978-1492883074
ISBN-10: 1492883077

United States Copyright Office: 1-1003688701
BISAC: Fiction / Visionary & Metaphysical

Mom
Wife
Witch

Jay Buckner

Jay Buckner

Prologue

It was impossible for the girl not to smile when she heard her kidnapper's gentle knock. She turned to see him slowly push the unlocked door open with his foot, holding her dinner tray in his hands.

They'd had a fun afternoon including a leisurely mini-buffet luncheon in the sunroom catered and delivered by her favorite Chinese restaurant. Then the man financed a matinee at the movies, taxi and unlimited snacks included, which may have been the reason she went to the art theatre to see the original of "The Girl With The Dragon Tattoo" for the third time. Lately she couldn't satisfy that sweet tooth of hers and he frowned upon bringing sugars into the house. She tried to get him to accompany her but he declined again, as usual. That they had never left the house together didn't bother the girl anymore than her disguise when out and about. She understood.

The spontaneous smile with which she greeted him as he entered the room was genuine. She couldn't help but be happy when she saw the man. But this day the girl was unable hide the peek of sadness that escaped her being and seeped into the air between them. She wasn't a good actor though they'd discussed the coming of this day for months. The girl didn't want to leave, not ever.

She had awakened that morning to see him carefully placing the complementary skirt and blouse at the foot of the bed, the clothes she had shopped for and selected herself from the finest store in the town, very dressy and expensive attire for the return home to her parents she thought but he had insisted. She needed new clothes anyway as she had gained weight since she first arrived.

He was wearing gloves when he placed her new clothes at the foot of the bed, still protected within the store wrapping. The gloves may have been out of the ordinary even for him but anything he did was fine with her.

The girl was thinking she'd never tire looking at the man though she'd never seen his face. He always wore the mask. She had no idea what he really looked like or who he was. For the first few weeks they were together she was terrified of him but she got over that. Now she could no longer remember a time when she didn't love him. It had been six months since he'd kidnapped her. But that wasn't enough. She wanted more.

And he loved her. Their parting pained him as much as it did her. He loved all of them in his way. As with the others, he'd given her everything he could to set her course and now it was time to let her go.

The day was too short for the girl. When the hour came she showered, then opened the clothes wrappings and donned new everything, stepped into slippers she'd never seen before and stood waiting near the entrance as he'd asked. A limousine arrived precisely at 8:00 pm. At the front door she exchanged the slippers for the shoes he'd bought for her and reluctantly left his house for the last time and stepped into the waiting car, looking back at the closed door hoping to catch one more glimpse of him.

Gracie Hanson was then driven back home to her grieving parents who had been praying for six months that their daughter might someday be found alive.

By 9:00 PM the man had completely vacated the house, methodically removing any possible sign that he had ever been there; not a hair, not a fingerprint was left. He then drove through the black night until he arrived at the next house he would occupy for the following eight months, and start all over again. Police cars arrived at the empty house by 10 pm.

Chapter 1

The day before, a terrified middle-aged man threw himself through the entrance of a police station and confessed to an unsolved series of molestations, pleading to be taken into custody.

Two detectives and a Child Protection Agency advocate were now huddled in a small room trying to figure out what to do with the woman they were certain had information that could help unravel the mystery as to what frightened the pervert into confessing. His wasn't the first bizarre instance of a deviant begging for incarceration. During the preceding four years there were more than a dozen cases throughout the state of Washington with a similar story. It appeared there were vigilantes at work, maybe a gang doing a better job than the police and one of the detectives had more than a hunch that the woman, a local artist, was in the middle of it.

"Says her name is Stanich," said Lou Pasquale, the taller of the detectives.

"She's lying. She's Packard. And she knows more than she's saying," said Stanley Millman, the shorter of the two but with more hair, which is why he referred to his partner as Samson when he wanted to irritate Lou on slow days when mandatory male bonding called for ribbing. Stanley was always Stanley, never Stan.

"Maybe, but Packard was blonde, with glasses. And the nose was bigger," said Pasquale.

"She faked it on the California license. I'm telling you she's Packard. She's the one."

"Two licenses 17 years apart here in Washington say she's Stanich. She deliberately changed her name and face in the middle? Why?"

"Beats me. Maybe she got married and changed her mind about the name thing. Maybe she had an accident or plastic surgery. And the husband who claims he's Jack Stanich did the same thing. The black Packard and the white Stanich are the same man I'm telling you."

"Not black...maybe a deep tan, beard, glasses...I don't see how you can prove he's the same man. What about those kids?"

"Santa Cruz came up blank. No pictures, no prints, no nothing."

"School pictures?"

"Seems the Packard kids were always somewhere else when photos were taken."

"Something really weird's going on here. Okay, let's do this another way. Separate them, the parents in one room and the kids in another. Any objection?" Pasquale said to the advocate.

"Not as long as I'm with them," he replied.

"Joining us for the duration, yes?"

"Sleep in their cell if I have to."

"No one's talking detention," said Millman.

The detectives and the advocate walked down the corridor and into the room where the woman was waiting with her husband and children, a boy and an older girl, all chuckling about something. As they entered the laughter stopped, except for the boy. The grin never left his face as he picked up a camera and took their picture. The family smiled at him, except the girl who was buried in a book.

"You can't do that here," said Millman. "Not permitted. We'll have to hold on to that camera."

"No film, no memory card. See for yourself," said the boy, and continued to take empty pictures until the camera was taken away.

"Look, you're entitled to a lawyer," said Pasquale, addressing the woman. "Why make this harder on yourself?"

"That's exactly how we see it," she said. "We decline our right to an attorney. We will be our own counsel. Pro se works for us and makes it easier on you. You deal directly with the source, me. Now, what do you want?"

"Okay, fine, we're going to question each of you separately," said Pasquale.

"Don't be silly," she said. "Are we under arrest? No. We're here just to do you a favor. Don't push it. We stay together until we decide we've had enough and then we leave, unless you want to arrest my 12-year-old son on suspicion of suspicion."

"Very funny. Ma'am...Susan, Jack, Patricia and Max are the Packard names. You're the Packards. I know it," said Millman, taking his turn in their game of good cop, good cop.

"Prove it. Fellas, my children's names aren't special, except to me. There must be millions of girls named Patricia, and just about as many Max's. More than 3,200 are in the same family, 27 with parents that share our names. How come they're not here?"

"Plucking numbers out of the air is cute but it doesn't change a thing," said Pasquale; his turn.

"They weren't plucked out of the air," said Jack Stanich, speaking for the first time since they were brought in. The detectives and the advocate looked at the man, then the woman. She smiled back. The boy laughed. The girl kept reading her book.

"Look, lady – "

Susan cut the taller of the detectives off – "Susan....Susan Stanich...Ms. or Mrs. Stanich....pick one but cut the 'lady' crap." All the while Susan kept stroking the folded barber's razor in her pocket that never left her person when out and about, a relic from an earlier life, a tic of sorts.

"Okay, okay...look," said Pasquale, "we got a crazy, Lawrence Compton, whose prints match a molester we've been trying to catch for six years. He's petrified of you and begging us to keep him locked up. He swears he saw you flying through the air. We had to put him in a straightjacket."

"It's all in his mind," said Susan Stanich and began laughing and couldn't stop. The boy joined her in giggles. Jack Stanich looked on the detective with compassion. And the girl kept reading.

Stanley glared at Lou. It had been his turn.

Four years prior in a condo on the outskirts of Seattle a man was rushing about a morning routine that usually began by 5:00 am, not later than 6:00, allowing four maybe five hours of sleep. The perpetual adrenaline drip that was his norm wouldn't allow more. Dan Ramon had only one state of mind, obsession. Everything he did fed his obsession. Work, sleep, food...all of it only served to feed the addiction. The circles under his eyes attested to the 18 hours a day he sat in front of a computer staring at images of naked minors in a variety of poses and sex acts. Those activities that required attention outside of the object of his obsession were dispatched with military precision. He frequented the same 7/11 for the two packs of cigarettes he smoked each day, and the same 24-hour supermarket to fill gaps in groceries for breakfasts and dinners. The identical luncheon fare was always ordered from a nearby Chinese restaurant.

Each day was a mirror image of the day before, except that morning. When he left the supermarket a woman was standing outside the entrance as though waiting for him. As he passed she said, "Hi Dan." When he turned to look at her she was walking away. That was different, very different. It left him with an unsettling creep in the back of his neck.

At precisely the same time each day he sat in front of his computer. On that day he began an e-mail exchange he hoped would net him downloaded images from a new acquaintance he thought was in Thailand. He'd never met the man, didn't know his name other than the alias used in a chatroom. They'd both subscribed to a Thai website that offered a unique portal to individuals willing to pay a very high price for admission to that special site. The Terms of Use clearly stated that the images on the site were of youthful, consenting adults. That was a lie, just as the site was a front for a meeting ground where deviants could encounter others of a like bent. Nevertheless, it was virtually impossible for Thai authorities to close the site without being able to prove that the participants in the images were underage. But the *models* were nowhere to be found and usually masked.

Thai police weren't the only ones stymied by the disclosure and mask ruse. Investigative teams in more than a dozen countries were also on to the site and having an equally hard time cracking the child porn ring for the same reasons. Once subscribers exchanged private e-mail addresses they were lost in internet land without just cause to force the site to disclose credit card info to trace them. For the man in Seattle it was a moot point. The Thai man with whom he had been exchanging e-mails wasn't in Thailand, and he wasn't Thai, not even a man.

Ramon made the acquaintance of the individual the week before. Mutual paranoia dictated a careful screening before the exchange of explicit photos. The Thai was more cautious than most insisting that he be provided something graphic first before pouring his library into e-mails with a stranger. The bargaining for the trade was part of the excitement for Ramon, the unknown fueling further enticement to his expectations. The two did the innuendo dance up and back for several days but finally Ramon's craving drove him to e-mail the first image in heated anticipation of what he would receive in return. Yet even as he hit the send button the woman who had addressed him at the supermarket continued hovering on the back of his neck, but that red flag was overridden by compulsion.

It is possible that the *models* on the Thai site were of the age of consent but other images on the Ramon's hard drive would have been more than enough to convict him of possessing and distributing child pornography. Though privacy statutes prevented police from snooping for the purpose of entrapment without just cause, that restriction didn't necessarily hold for private citizens with a talent for hacking. That morning the image Ramon e-mailed was opened on a computer near Bellingham, Washington, little more than an hour from Ramon's condo. Susan Stanich viewed the file to be sure of the content and deleted it. She then made notations in a folder labeled 'Dan Ramon'. Vigilante justice was at work, but it wasn't a gang. She worked alone.

Susan Stanich had no use for anything electric. There were no overhead lines near the Stanich house. Before moving in and at her direction Jack Stanich obtained the necessary permits and paid to have the power moved to a utility pole 50 yards from their front door and then channeled underground through a heavily insulated duct. The Stanichs used electricity only for absolute basics such as washer/dryer and refrigerator, and the minimal lighting Susan insisted upon. There were no TVs or other electric appliances. So when Susan bought a computer and had it hooked into a DSL connection Jack Stanich thought it rather odd, completely out of character. Naturally, the children glommed on to the prospects the new computer presented to them. They asked, begged, pleaded. Susan said no in her customary sweet way. And that was that. Jack kept wondering what his wife was up to but wondering was as far as he got. His wife thought it best to keep him in the dark as to her new hobby. Besides, Jack enjoyed wondering, one of his favorite pastimes.

Ramon's addiction required a constant feeding of new images to keep in check the anxiety that would immediately fill the gaps between perverse rushes, and then only briefly. After sending his image to who he thought was a man in Thailand Ramon anxiously sat at his computer and waited for a reciprocal response, practically drooling in anticipation. He sat and waited, for hours. He would've waited for days but Susan didn't think that was necessary. She wasn't just toying with Ramon, preparing him was more like it. Dan Ramon didn't know it but he was being stalked and about to find that out.

After receiving his image Susan Stanich went shopping, leisurely, fully aware that Ramon was fast on the hook, her easy pace inversely proportional to his need to rush – the more anxious the prey, the slower her pace. That would magnify the first shock she would deliver to paranoid heights, precisely what she intended.

Susan delivered that surprise four hours into the exchange. When Dan Ramon saw the return response in his inbox his heart skipped a beat and began pumping faster. Now that the trade was in the bag he savored the moment, consciously trying to calm himself, slow his breathing. This was the moment for which he waited and brought to a brake all need to rush so as to fully relish the high.

Then he clicked on the e-mail. The attachment was there waiting for him but the file was unusually large for a single image. 'Shit' he thought, 'this will take minutes to download'. The pot of gold was nudged just a bit out of his momentary reach, seeming to tease him – shock management to an art form. He clicked on the attachment and sat there irritated that he would have to wait so long, his obsession now feeding on itself in a vacuum, almost bursting. After several excruciatingly slow moments the "Allow" window popped up. 'At last,' he thought and clicked "Yes," eyes widened, heart pumping. And the image flew open.

Instead of feeding on the picture of an unfortunate child he was greeted with a full, face-on photo of Susan Stanich looking directly at him, the woman who had been waiting for him at the supermarket. He stopped breathing. His face exploded in paranoia as cold as an Arctic grave. The freeze dripped down his head until it filled his toes and every inch between. The woman was on to him.

Ramon's mind went white blind, frozen in fear. The paralysis lasted only seconds and then the man began a frantic deletion of the files that could land him in jail. His brain roared with the details of what had to be done to cleanse his environment of any trace of child pornography. He dug into the digital folders within folders holding the thousands of images he had gathered on his hard drive over the years, dragging them into one folder that he then dumped into the trash icon. The dialog box indicated it would take an hour to delete. He then went to his e-mail and began deleting every message, Inbox and Sent, page by page. That took more than an hour. The trash dialog box was still deleting when he finished. There wasn't much in the way of printed hard copy, the one precaution he had been careful to employ. He gathered what there was from his bookshelf, stepped out of his apartment and buried the lot in the dumpster of an adjoining condo.

When he returned to his condo the trash dialog box was gone. But the files of porn he thought he had deleted were back on the computer's desktop. Ramon began scratching at his face. He again gathered the files and folders and this time individually placed them in the trash and watched each folder disappear from the desktop. Satisfied that they were being deleted he gathered the rest in one folder and again placed the lot in the trash icon. Disturbed and fearing the worst he then checked his e-mail. The e-mails were also back. He again dumped the e-mails, then opened the Administrator page and closed the account. Lastly, he grabbed a small tool box, shut down the computer and removed the hard drive, took it outside and smashed it on the pavement.

While Ramon was occupied destroying evidence, Susan Stanich decided the sweater she'd purchased as a reward for her good deed wasn't merited and returned it, fully aware that shopping as a pastime usually results in buying something you don't need until you see it. But sometimes Susan can be a girly girl and as such loves to shop, a genetic thing. In her case she enjoyed returning items almost as much as buying them, as though the refunds were new found savings. Besides, the only world she wanted to impress was her children and Jack and he preferred her without clothes.

A week went by before the next shock was delivered by way of a certified letter. Ramon signed for it with sweating hands, trembling slightly. His solitary life of perpetual paranoia precluded relationships with neighbors and any remaining family abandoned him years before, and he them. Friends were out of the question and his preoccupation left no room for casual acquaintances. Ramon received mail from no one ever. He knew the letter couldn't be anything good and anticipated the worst. He set the envelope on the kitchen table and sat himself down looking at it, finally got up his courage and opened it. The contents nicely fed his paranoia. The envelope was empty.

Then his phone rang, which it never did because no one had his unlisted number. The landline was necessary for the internet connection, that's all. His existence, other than bills and notices, was completely unknown. On rare occasions a telemarketer cruising with an auto-dialer might stumble upon his number, but the grip of rational terror told him that would not be the case this time.

He wouldn't answer, just kept staring at the phone. But it wouldn't stop ringing. The longer it rang the more he sweated, the deeper his dread. Then it stopped. But he continued looking at the phone, stuck. Even though he expected it, when the phone began ringing again it was a jolt. His mind began fragmenting. He would do anything to stop the ringing. So he answered.

"Did you get my little package?" a woman's voice on the other end asked.

"What do you want?" he screamed into the phone.

"You know what I want," she said.

"It's gone. All of it," he yelled into the receiver.

"What's gone?" she said. "Tell me. What's gone?"

"What do you want?" he repeated.

"Children are crying. Do you know that? You know why they're crying, don't you?" And she hung up.

He dropped the receiver on to the cradle and sat down and began bawling like a baby with his head in his hands, rocking back and forth.

The next day he received another envelope, this time with a message:

> *If the police catch you with the goods you go to jail. By now you know I can make that happen. You know what they do to with a cho-mo in prison, don't you? You'll never get out alive. Go to the police before they come to you. You're going to tell them what you are and ask to be put in the sexual predator database. I know you can't help what you feel but we'll help you control how you act. If I ever suspect you are at it again. I'll make sure you go to jail and never get out. I'll always be watching you. Go to the police now, right now.*

Several photos of castrated men accompanied the letter.

Then the phone rang. He answered it on the second ring. No one was there. Within the hour a red-eyed Dan Ramon walked into a police station and confessed. He was her first.

The two detectives and Susan Stanich were standing in the corridor outside the room while the rest of her family remained inside waiting on them. Pasquale had asked Susan if they could talk to her alone, saying he thought it best if her children were not involved. Sure, why not.

Susan Stanich may be considered beautiful by some, though not classically pretty because she has a majorly crooked nose with a nice bump on it, a remnant from a rough childhood. The woman is both elegant and street at the same time with an imposing physical presence, powerfully sleek, almost feline, a tough cookie with glowing clear skin and piercing blue-blue eyes, one of the lucky few who will probably look just as good at sixty or eighty, ageless. More than smart and quick witted, she not only remembers everything but knows what to do with the information she's given, graced with generous access to wisdom, insight and intelligence, all in all a fortunate woman blessed with abundance. But it wasn't always that way.

"Does the name Dan Ramon strike a chord?" said Millman. "Four years ago you drove him into our arms. Search your memory."

"Let me think about it," said Susan.

"Compton and Ramon have both ID'd you. We got you. If you insist we'll bring in another half dozen deviants and I'll give you 10 to 1 they all ID you. You gonna make me do that, hah?"

"Sure, go ahead," said Susan. Then what? You think you'll have something? Even if I did everything you say and I am Susan Packard you still have nothing. I know it. You know it, unless you want to tell a judge I fly through the air on a broomstick. Now, what do you want?"

Pasquale: "Ms. Stanich, or Packard, whoever you are or whatever name you want to go by, we got a bad one this time. He steals girls and keeps them. Months later they show up in another city or state. When he's done with them they're changed. Their childhood's gone."

"He?" she said. "You're so sure it's a he...could be a she that looks like a he."

Millman looked at Pasquale, who hesitated a long minute, then Millman nodded and said "Tell her."

"Ms. Stanich, the kidnapped girls are all come back pregnant and happy, almost blissful, uncooperative without exception. He holds them long enough to make an abortion by reason of rape impossible, not that any of the girls would've gone along with that. Five of them have borne his children over the past seven years. They keep their babies. Maybe you can give us some insight into what we dealing with so we can catch this guy. We got nothing except maybe his DNA, that is if any of the victims ever give us permission to take an admissible swab, which they haven't so far."

"That's why I'm here? You think I know something about Narcissistic Personality Disorder? Why did you drag my family along for this? What do they know?"

"Narcissistic Personality Disorder?" said Pasquale.

"Of course," said the woman. "Don't you know? I thought you were the detective. Bit of a variation but that's what it smells like to me."

"Ma'am, this is about kidnapped children being forced to have babies. We know your daughter's history. We know about the kidnapping and what happened, what she did. We hoped you'd be more sympathetic if your children came along for the ride. You know what it feels like to have your child kidnapped. We need your help."

"We don't need yours. We didn't then and we don't now. Fucking police just got in the way. I work alone. But thanks for the tip."

"Then it is you," said Pasquale. "Ms. Stanich, we got you on a dozen flavors of blackmail, vigilantism, identity and mail fraud, breaking and entering..."

"Gentlemen, c'mon, I thought we just agreed you got nothing. I guarantee I have an alibi for everything you thought you had. You haven't got a thing except a bunch of hysterical perverts you couldn't stop until someone helped them stop themselves. Makes you wonder about their fit of self control, doesn't it? You actually think you can prosecute me for stopping child porn? Look, you got nothing so cut the threats. You're just gonna irritate me. Whattaya say?"

Millman tried: "Ms. Stanich, we're drawing a blank on this. We don't know how you get under the skin of these people but if there's any way you can help us stop this...psycho....you have an accent. You're not from the northwest or California, are you? Back east, right? Him too," he added, pointing at Pasquale.

"How come this hasn't been in the news?" she asked, ignoring the question. "I keep up on these things, a hobby. How come I never heard about these girls?"

Millman: "They've been taken all over the northwest and chalked up as runaways. No one connected the dots until now. Lou picked up the pattern from police blotters, uncooperative runaways who wouldn't talk when they came back home pregnant, not that it's all that rare, but this bunch are calm, peaceful, delighted. Some of the parents still think there's a boyfriend somewhere in the picture. No way, this is the work of one nut."

"I tried to interview them and got nowhere," said Pasquale. "But what they didn't say and their denials were identical. There's a kidnapper out there who thinks he's a white knight of some kind."

"White knight, bullshit," said Susan. She looked at the officers then down at the floor. The three of them stood there in silence while she weighed her thoughts, then looked Lou carefully and slowly right in his eyes, up close so he would know it's serious time."This stupidity can't be why I'm here. Something else is going on. I can smell it." There was a long pause as she measured her thoughts. The cops waited on her. "Okay, let's do this. Why not? What do you have? I want to see everything and talk to the girls he's impregnated. Absolutely no one is ever to know I'm involved, ever. And you're paying for my round-trip airfare to New York."

"Well, that's...um....okay. Am I allowed to inquire as to why New York?" said Pasquale.

"That's where I come from, The Bronx. There's a few graves there I'd like to talk to. So, now you know everything. Feel better? Where's my fucking broomstick?"

Jack Stanich patiently sat inside the room with his children waiting for his wife to convince the detectives they were barking up the wrong tree. The advocate casually leaned against the wall asking vanilla questions about the children's schools, friends, hobbies, once in a while sneaking in a probe about their mother that the children parried with silence under their father's approving nod, at which point the thwarted advocate would return to vanilla, and then try again of course.

"It's probably a case of mistaken identity. Happens all the time," he said.

"No, I don't think so," said Patricia, singing the comment at him, finally bored just humoring the advocate, which earned a glare from Jack Stanich, but that didn't stop her. Mrs. Stanich provided a solid, stand-up role model for her 16-year-old daughter, offering genes with fearless eyes, though her mother's are bright blue while Patricia's are an unusual light brown, comparably intense yet equally pleasant when not aimed in anger.

"You don't think it is mistaken identity?" asked the advocate.

"Nope," said the girl.

"Patricia, shut up," said her father.

"Too late. Mom's going to help them. And she's going to New York."

Jack Stanich, formerly Packard, and his twelve-year-old son Max looked at Patricia. The advocate wondered why the girl made such an odd statement.

A moment later Susan Stanich and the two detectives entered the room and informed the family about her new project only to discover they already seemed to know. Susan Stanich put a long hard look on her daughter, at which point Patricia opened her book and returned to reading until her parents dragged her out of the police station for the trip back home. Alas, Patricia had been two pages shy of the chapter end, a real cliff hanger. That made the ride with her most unpleasant as she was uncomfortable reading in a moving car and thus left in a state of want that she gladly shared with the rest of the family, and offered them her discomfort as performance art.

Back at their desks the two detectives were trying to decipher the events of the day for their report in some way that would make sense.

"Okay Lou, genius, how do we expense this?"

"You know she's right. We really don't have her on anything. Seeing as how this is going that could make her an informant, right?"

"Yeah, I guess that's one way of looking at it. I sure wouldn't want to get on that woman's bad side."

"One strange family, huh?"

"Ya think!"

Chapter 2

Over the past several years it became increasingly apparent that someone else had been doing a better job than the police just by scaring the living shit out of criminal deviants. Now that the cat was out of the bag Pasquale was determined to figure out how Susan Stanich did it so he could add her MO to his repertoire. Lou Pasquale didn't know it but banging his head against a wall would've made just as much sense.

Ms. Stanich declined Pasquale's invitation to make use of an empty desk at the precinct, little disturbed by his obvious attempt to bring her close so he could discover how she tracked felons, which she knew would only divert him from the task at hand.

She wanted to be left alone to fill the three days before departing to New York with absolutely nothing. She refused to take the files Millman insisted she review. Nor did she show up as a guest informant for the briefing that had been arranged on her behalf with detectives working on the case. For three days Susan didn't even cook, clean or run errands, which completed her desire for nothing. She did e-mail Lou as a courtesy: "Thanks for the ticket. I'll let you know when I get back." That was the last they heard from her for weeks. But she was working, creating empty spaces in her mind so that her spirit could do its work. That was her way. Jack Stanich had seen her like this many times before and so assumed her chores and let her be.

The three days prior to Ms. Stanich's departure were as peaceful and uneventful as intended until Patricia showed up by way of a bedroom door deliberately left very ajar. Inside was her daughter stuffing a suitcase

"Where do you think you're going?" said Susan.

"I want come to New York with you."

"This isn't a sightseeing trip."

"You're going to talk with dead people, like in the movie?"

"If you think dead people talk I obviously didn't hit you enough when you were little. It's my fault that you're a moron."

"You have to stop calling me a moron. When do we have to be at the airport?" said Patricia. And so it was that daughter was to join mother. Stinging banter was typical of their conversation, a teenage daughter thing. Even good morning greetings were laced with snappy volley and comeback. Losing appropriate arguments when it made sense was Susan's way of building her child's character. Appropriately enough, Susan would draw a firm line when one of her children made a choice in which they might be physically or emotionally incapable of safe navigation, flying lessons that erred on the side of caution. Susan was fiercely protective as all mothers are but had additional tools at her disposal. Max's education for the most part was left to Jack, or so they thought.

Lou Pasquale looked terrific: suit, tie, and haircut. You'd never suspect he was a cop except for his darting eyes and the way he looked the restaurant over, or how he sat with his back to the wall instead of deferring to common courtesy as a gentleman and offer his attractive date the view, insisting that she be the one seen by the other patrons. Though she was hot he was still a 24-hour cop, every bit as subtle as an illuminated badge, the bulge of his required sidearm barely noticeable unless you looked in his direction.

Pasquale knew his blind date was a good one because he was nervous. So he tried to convince himself she was only just okay in an effort to keep from losing his poise. But himself came back at Pasquale and made sure he stayed rattled. Indeed, she was a good one. As a result he was very confused throughout the wine, desperately fighting off a mid-life flashback to awkward youth, trying not to let the wine dribble down his chin when it got stuck in the lump in his throat.

He made it to the finale of the salad and soup tests without saying anything with too much grovel or police-like. That gave Pasquale some confidence but not enough to invite himself to the party quite yet. He was still hiding in someone else, probably an assortment of Brad Pitt and Sylvester Stallone moves, with some Meryl Streep thrown in for the requisite feminine side. He loved movies, movies and kids.

Pasquale got lucky when his date suddenly sneezed just before the entree was served. The timing was provident because the sneeze was an embarrassingly messy one and she knew he caught a glimpse. See-saw, presto, she was as nervous as Pasquale. His date was only human and just like that he became Pasquale again, saved by a sneeze, his power returned. The night was going to be a good one. He just knew it. Then his phone rang and it changed his mind.

She watched as he listened on the cell. His faced dropped a little, the glow started fading, and then she saw the beginning of the metamorphosis to detective showing up in his focus, intensity. Within seconds there was a complete change in his countenance. She was intrigued by the result. As far as his date was concerned Pasquale looked pretty good either way, both before and after copness. So the night didn't work out the way they thought yet ended up the way they had hoped. They each liked what they saw.

"I'm terribly sorry but I must go," said Pasquale.

"Can't tell me why, huh?" asked the date.

"Can we do this again?" he asked.

"When?" she said, and smiled, a big one. He couldn't switch back to 'not-cop' fast enough to return her smile but she could see in his eyes that this was going to be fun. His date's name is Janice Goldman, or Dr. Goldman the gynecologist. Lou really scored big. She'll be with us from time to time to help calm Pasquale down after a conversation with Susan Stanich.

Their goodbye was more like hello. First there were pecks on the cheeks and then the excuse of a gentle handshake to let them feel each other's touch, then another peck on the other cheek but with added linger this time, lastly eye contact full of promise.

Once they concluded 'hello' Pasquale was out of there and headed to the precinct to meet the very pregnant child-woman Gracie Hanson and her sincerely grateful, relieved, angry, shocked parents. On the drive over he called Susan Stanich and invited her to join them during the interrogation. She recognized his voice and hung up. Didn't hurt to try.

Lt. Detective Pasquale didn't have children of his own, which may explain why he suffered a very peculiar fascination. He adored babies, toddlers, from the time they could smile, like a moth to a flame. It seemed once a week Lou would pull the car over in the middle of nowhere, get out of the car flashing his badge and a great big smile, and ask some startled mother if he could say hello to her baby. He just loved them. The mother would go through a variation of the five stages of grief: Caution, Puzzlement, Acceptance, Wonder, and Amusement...a big guy like that laughing with a baby. He just adored them, every one of them. And absolutely nothing made the hair on the back of his neck stand up more than someone bringing harm to a child. That was Lou Pasquale's best side.

Stanley Millman, his partner, was cursed with proximity and therefore innocent by association, constantly embarrassed by Lou's idiosyncrasy. "You want a kid? I got extra," was Millman's refrain every time he had to suffer alongside a kitchy koo attack as his eccentric partner introduced himself to another two-year-old. Millman's interest in children only began when they were old enough to debate him. He barely recognized his own offspring before then, a boy and girl who considered him a stranger until he convinced them otherwise during an argument that he lost with his five-year-old son. Stanley Millman was a softy.

Pasquale was the tough guy of the duo, a real one, which meant he had no need to engage in macho posturing to telegraph menace so as to keep real or imagined threats at bay, not even a hint of swagger. He wore neither worry nor fear and that relaxed confidence was clearly visible in his easy eyes. Like many men and women with a secure core he spoke carefully and softly, compelling listeners to be attentive, more so than less centered individuals with a need for drama or volume; small dog syndrome. A transplant to the Seattle area, he'd grown up in The Bronx, a coincidence not lost on Susan Stanich once she heard his accent, though he initially had trouble placing hers because she wanted it that way

Pasquale outgrew his neighborhood off the Grand Concourse in his early twenties after a tour as a marine during the first Iraq conflict. He came back convinced of the soul's inevitable destruction as a result of war and violence and made a deliberate choice to dedicate his life to confronting aggression, which may seem to be an oxymoron but it's not. Pasquale moved to the northwest and became a cop. A decade or so later he was one of the first Iraq war veterans in the forefront of voices protesting Iraq war redux. Now, another decade later, he was a decorated detective on the Seattle police force. He had the pick of assignments and chose the capture of felons whose criminal acts harmed children: kidnappers, molesters, abusers. He figured the most damage was inflicted on a human at the earliest stages of life and that was where, by stopping it, he could do the most good. There was no troubled childhood of neglect to explain Pasquale's devotion to preventing abuse. By good fortune it's just the way he's made.

Pasquale was stopped in his tracks upon entering the room, completely thrown off by the sight of a beautiful young woman who practically glowed, eating ice cream like a kid.

"Lt. Detective Pasquale I'd like you to meet Gracie Hanson," said Millman.

She looked great, well dressed and in obvious excellent health, slurping the cone. Her thankful parents wouldn't let her out of their sight and stood guard on either side on their pregnant daughter, with stares fixed on their found child, probably trying to figure out what to do with her next.

Tipped off police had been watching the Hanson house when the limousine pulled up to the curb barely an hour earlier. Two uniformed officers and Ms. Hanson's parents watched the girl exit the car and came rushing at her from two directions, scaring the hell out of Gracie. "Get off me," she yelled at the cops talking too close to her face, but allowed her parents to smother her. "Look, Mom," the girl said to her mother, pointing at her belly, "Baby." "Oh, my God," said her mother. Gracie gave her a great big smile. By the time they arrived at the precinct she was hugged out, her clothes were wet from the mother's tears, and both parents couldn't hide their wonderment at the complete stranger who was once their daughter.

Gracie Hanson stopped licking her cone when Pasquale entered, gawking at her. She looked Pasquale over and then informed him, "I'm not telling you anything that can help you find the man. But you can ask. You will anyway. I'm ready."

"We can hold you as a material witness for a long time," said Stanley.

"Okay, but that's bull. I didn't kidnap me. I'm the victim, remember?" she replied.

"You may be withholding knowledge of the kidnapper that can help us catch him. That is a felony."

"Well, I'm not. I'll answer everything you ask but nothing I can tell you will help you find the man. I don't know what he looks like, his name or where he is. Go ahead, ask me. I'll tell you what I know. It ain't much. Make me take a lie detector. See for yourself."

Lou jumped in, "I understand you could have walked away at any time."

"Yes," she said. "So what, what law did I break? I was under his spell. I still am. I always will be. Is that a crime?"

Then Millman said to Pasquale, as though she weren't even in the room, "She can't stop talking about him but says nothing. And she knows the law. She's been prepped for this. Go ahead, give it a try. I'll watch." Gracie couldn't help but smile.

Pasquale: "You realize that what this man did to you amounts to kidnap and rape."

"Of course, that's the law. Do I look like an idiot?" she replied.

"Do you know where you were for the past six months? Could you take us there?"

"Better than that," she said. "I'll give you the address, but he's gone."

"How old would you say he was?"

"I don't know. I never saw his face."

"Would you recognize his voice if you heard it again?"

"Absolutely. I can still hear him in my head."

"You must have seen his arms or legs. There had to be some distinguishing marks, something."

"Nope. He seemed to be in good shape but not one of those musclemen. Nice body." Her parents winced; more information than they needed to hear.

"What name did you call him? He must have given you a name."

"He didn't. I just talked to him like you're talking to me and your friend over there," she said, pointing to Millman.

"He's a man. That's all I know." It was a dead end. All the victims said the same thing, almost verbatim.

"I know what all of you think and you're wrong," she said. "He didn't tell me what to say, not ever. He wasn't like that. But we often talked about what would happen when I got home. This is so sad....go ahead, ask me more questions. I'll tell you everything I know. He was terrific, a very nice man. I love him. If you knew him you'd like him. Can I go back home now? I'm hungry." Then to her parents: "Can we stop at a restaurant, but not Chinese? I had that for lunch."

Her parents' shock deepened with each response she gave. Their daughter had definitely changed and they weren't sure if it were for better or worse. Before the kidnapping she was still their little girl. Now it seemed she skipped a decade or so and had suddenly become her own person, and in a few months she would make them grandparents.

The conversation was basically the same each time Pasquale and Millman interrogated one of the kidnapped girls. The kidnapper had picked smart, mature girls. They seemed well-adjusted to begin with, not susceptible, gullible or needy as psychological profiles might suggest, rather open-minded to accepting the skewed view of the world the kidnapper presented as perfectly acceptable. As far as each was concerned he was kind, sensible, and intelligent. Police and parents saw his effect on the girls as brilliant brainwashing, but not Susan Stanich. She would have a very different take on matters.

"When is that Stanich woman coming back?" Pasquale said to Millman.

"You have a wait. She hasn't even left yet," replied his shorter partner, which Pasquale already knew. Stymied, he was just venting.

Pasquale felt certain Susan Stanich could get the victims to talk. No one else could and they seemed to speak the same language; condescendingly polite spiced with a cutting disrespect for his authority, maybe any authority. Talking to the victims was as difficult as dealing with Stanich. In spite of their age the kidnapped young women were formidable, stubbornly certain of their place in the world and comfortable in their own skin. To compound Pasquale's frustration they became responsible, loving mothers. The detective found it all very confusing.

Chapter 3

As they stepped from the plane Patricia could sense a difference in her mother.

After more than two decades in the west Susan Stanich began the return to the only place in the world where she felt completely at home: The Bronx. None of us can cast off our history regardless of how successful we are in re-creating ourselves. We carry that legacy forever. As such, Susan's roots remain deep. White Castle hamburgers, hot dog stands and New York pizza were mother's milk. The oppressive, Summers heat and humidity are welcome, familiar.

Susan could visit but knew she could never again stay. She no longer belonged. Few natives ever return once they leave, yet upon each New York City leaves an indelible imprint. The young woman who once went by the nickname Knife was back, if only for a brief time.

There is just one New York and it's a serious place, filling the senses to impress upon inhabitants and visitors alike that a gritty Oz does exist. Sidewalks and streets have history as well as a future with ancient odors stirred into an omnipresent hum of activity filled with promise. Smart ambitious people from every country in the world rush about fulfilling lifelong dreams with intensity you can practically feel on the skin. Electricity races through the air painting inhabitants with purpose and direction.

The mother daughter cabbed towards the Manhattan night in silence. Susan's heart was pounding as the most painful of her memories began surfacing for the dead she'd left behind decades before. She always knew the day would come when she'd have to see their faces again and set things straight. This was that day.

Patricia was spellbound by the massive center of the universe as the city drew closer and lights from streets, homes and businesses turned night into day in every direction without a gap.

"Take the Brooklyn Bridge, not the tunnel," Susan said to the cabbie. "I want you to see the view," she added to Patricia, whose eyes got yet wider but were still unable to grasp the size of the illuminated skyline as it grew bigger than anything she could have imagined. That was all Susan said until they walked into the midtown hotel. Patricia said less.

When they stepped from the cab a side of her mother began emerging that Patricia had never seen before. Susan unconsciously lowered her head a bit and her shoulders became rounded, her back slightly hunched. She was less light-footed, cautiously scanning the people they passed almost like a predatory animal. Patricia gave her space, mesmerized by the transformation. But she was not done seeing the rest of her mother.

Then Susan began to speak. The sound of a mother's voice is without accent to her child. On occasion Susan would slip in a word or phrase with a slightly unfamiliar sound, yet not enough for her children to take notice. But at the hotel registration desk the accent and attitude with which Susan spoke sounded drastically different to her daughter, alien.

"Stanich," said Susan to the clerk at the registration desk, "dere's a reservation."

"Yes, ma'am, here it is," he said, "our deluxe room with a king-sized bed."

"Look again, Dudley" she said.

"Stanich. Deluxe room with a king-size bed. Here it is," repeated the clerk, pointing to a place on his monitor, putting forth his most welcoming smile.

"No, Dudley, dat ain't wat I ast for."

"My name is Paul."

"I don't give a fuck wat ya name is. Dat ain't wat I ast for."

For the first time in her life a stunned Patricia caught a glimpse of the teen-age Knife, the person who was once her mother. It took five minutes and some room juggling for a nervous shift manager to find the deluxe room with two queen size beds that Susan had reserved. But from that moment on and until they were back on the west coast Patricia would watch in wonder the change that had taken over her mother.

After dinner they settled into the well-appointed room, watched some TV and then went to sleep. Not a word passed between them. Susan wasn't ready. Neither was Patricia.

Several weeks before Gracie Hansen was returned to her parents the kidnapper was planning ahead, seated in a neighborhood theatre watching a high school production of "Much Ado About Nothing". He was unrecognizable wearing glasses and an expensive, expertly fit hair piece with matching mustache. The striking lead in the cast caught his eye. She was beautiful of course, but also confident and charismatic. Without any intentional upstaging, she easily stole the scene from the rest of the players. And her burgeoning talent was apparent, a bonus as her presence alone would have been enough to draw the air in the theatre to her radiant face. Dressing the girl down wouldn't have lessened the spotlight that fell upon her. And casting her in bit parts would cheat the audience. Some have it, she did. The kidnapper knew he need look no further. He had found the next one. Gracie could go home.

The man began checking the time at the beginning of the second act when Shakespeare's Beatrice explains why she will never marry. It disturbed the kidnapper that he would have to leave the play to make a phone call. Once he settled on the next victim he hated leaving her even for a moment, envious of the air she breathed unless he could breathe it with her.

Midway through the act, he reluctantly he tore himself from the sight of her form and left the theatre for the hour's drive ahead. She was on his mind the entire time, her face, the way she moved and spoke, becoming his sole preoccupation until he could see her next. But the call was important. Approximately once a month, he would drive an hour or two from wherever he was and make a pre-arranged call using a prepaid cell phone. The person on the other end would take the call at one of the few public phone booths still available. Throughout the year they used different days of the month, different times and different locations, setting up the next call at the end of each. They were untraceable.

The next morning Susan began the trip back in time to lighten the weight from her past life. She felt it appropriate that her daughter join her on the journey and so learn the chronicle of the maternal line Patricia was to inherit, confident of her daughter's capacity to absorb the hard stuff she would place on her plate in the days that would follow. Street life might be romanticized but it's not a pretty picture. Patricia would never become the creature that lived inside her mother yet was her double in many other ways. She could cope with reality.

Typical mother daughter wake-up chit-chat started the day same as every morning, as though the mystery person her mother had become the night before never happened: showers, outfits, breakfast and then out of there. "Where are we going?" Patricia said as they stepped into the cab.

"Potter's Field on Hart's Island. That's where her grave is." And to the driver: "Fordham Street, City Island, please." Susan had history with New York cab drivers. She liked them. Today they liked her: long drive, big fare, happy cabby.

"Whose grave?"

"Your grandmother, my mother. Potter's Field is the cemetery for people who were homeless or alone in death. On the island they have plenty of company."

"You told us you woke one morning and your mother was just dead. You were there."

"I had to leave her where she died. She would have wanted me to? The police found her. I called them," said Susan. "That's all you need to know for now."

"You're sure she's there?"

"There's a website, a database. Her name is listed."

"Do we have to go today, now?"

"I told you this is not a sightseeing trip. Visitors are allowed one Thursday a month. We have to go today."

"Do you know where her grave is?"

"No. I'm not sure anyone knows...but I'll find her. We'll find each other. We're in the air." Susan said, leaving no doubt that somehow she would. Patricia looked at her mother. The stranger from the night before was returning.

Access to Potter's Field has to be pre-arranged. Only family members are permitted. Susan had made the reservation via e-mail months before; the trip to New York was not the spur of the moment decision as it had appeared. Visitors are ferried by boat from an embarkation pier on City Island in The Bronx. It was on the taxi ride from Manhattan that Patricia began asking the questions that Susan knew she might someday have to answer.

"Tell me about the scars," said Patricia.

Until her children were three or so, Susan thought nothing of walking around naked in front of them assuming they would forget the scars on her breasts or think they were a distorted memory, maybe a dream. But Patricia remembered. "Scars?" said Susan as she closed the bullet-proof divider that separates the driver from passengers for safety and also provides some confidentiality if voices are kept low.

"Mom, you have scars on your breasts. How did they get there?"

Lying to avoid prematurely aging her daughter was tempting but the easy-out of dishonesty isn't available to people like Susan Stanich. So, she took a deep breath, looked her daughter in the eye and told her: "When I was your age men kidnapped me, pimps, men who live off the sale of women's bodies for sex. They beat me. That's why my nose is crooked. Then they raped me. When they were done one of them cut my breasts to ruin me so that no man would ever want me...but that didn't work now did it?"

Susan gave her daughter time to let the shock and its implications sink in. She could see the child's thinking; watch her daughter reluctantly settle on the obvious conclusion with disbelief, then observed Patricia's mind searching in vain for other possibilities.

"Did the police ever catch them?" Patricia asked in an effort to avoid confronting what she feared her mother would tell her next. She didn't want to know. Susan felt otherwise.

"No, Patricia. I did. I caught the one who cut me, just him." There was a long pause before Susan spoke next: "He never cut anyone again." The lethal implication of the last statement wasn't lost on her daughter. It pained Susan to see Patricia wrestling with brutal truths beyond anyone's years but she wanted her daughter to know. Her history had to be voiced. As she saw it, part of her job as a mother was to prepare her children for life, make sure they know and accept the world on its own terms. Susan Stanich doesn't do pollyanna. Straightforward was her style.

Patricia had been aware that her mother was unusual from an early age. They grew up with Susan's almost daily premonitions and photographic memory. Odd goings on were accepted in the household as commonplace. Sometimes she would disappear for as long as a day or two, returning only to sleep. When asked where she had gone Susan would always answer, "Out." But the extent of her extraordinary qualities Susan kept hidden from her daughter, just as they were concealed from little Max and Jack Stanich to a large extent. She wanted to shield her family from the burden of keeping secrets that could negatively affect their lives and possibly alter the path that was their destiny. She wanted her brood to live as ordinary a life as possible. Normal was good though it wasn't always in the cards for her family whom fate had marked for an uncommon, challenging journey.

Four years prior, when they were living in Santa Cruz and still the Packards, Patricia had been kidnapped by a madwoman, Eloise De Marco. Patricia managed to escape, which was remarkable by itself but that was only the half of it. Her kidnapping became a sensation mostly due to the circumstances under which the kidnapper was discovered. It seemed that when Patricia got the best of the insane woman she nailed her to the floor where the maniac was eventually found screaming incoherently. That was her state for the rest of the poor woman's life, babbling and foaming at the mouth, bellowing something about Patricia's eyes to her last breath barely two years after the abduction. Something made De Marco's mind completely snap and no one ever knew why, except Susan Stanich, who was intimately acquainted with more of that day's events. Patricia was never able to fully reveal how she overcame the woman. She had freed herself from the ropes that bound her with a knife but had no memory of overcoming the woman because it was Susan who confronted Eloise De Marco, as well as her daughter.

Susan's spirit slipped inside her kidnapped child as the girl was about to kill the woman with a knife and stopped her, and then Susan slipped back out and traveled somewhere else. She wasn't there to rescue Patricia but to save the maniac from her daughter's wrath. Susan Stanich is a witch, not a fairy tale witch or a literary creation like you think this is, but a real one. Just the same, the bit with nailing the madwoman to the floor was all Patricia.

Within days of the girl's return the Packards disappeared from Santa Cruz and showed up in Washington State as the

Stanich family a week later. Patricia cut and dyed her hair and wore great big black-rimmed glasses. It worked. The Packards had vanished, until now.

Like all mothers, even witches have limitations; their children. "Mom, why did those men cut you?" asked her daughter, having regained her balance and now, unfortunately for her mother, on a roll.

"I made the mistake of being in his part of the city, his neighborhood, his turf. He considered the girls who worked his streets his property."

"Mom – "

"Patricia....I was a prostitute...from the time I was about 12."

The girl was again struck speechless, her brain now reeling in an attempt to absorb information so far removed from anything she could comprehend as remotely possible. Nonetheless it was a non-negotiable truth. There was no need for anything further to be said, not yet, but she couldn't take her eyes off her new mother.

Hart's Island is oppressively bleak. Midnight cemetery creepiness blankets every blade of grass under the brightest mid-day sun, shoreline to shoreline in every direction, not the sort of place where the hardiest stalwart cynic would care to spend the night alone, rather a perfect camera-ready set for a horror movie. As the Stanichs stepped on the island even the air seemed foul, as though they were now breathing the breath of those long dead, and they were not welcome.

Visitors aren't permitted beyond a small designated area near an out-of-place gazebo. Permission is required to walk the grounds and then only when escorted by an official. In her application Susan used her birth certificate to prove kinship, one she'd obtained only recently for that purpose. In the same correspondence she included a letter asking to tour the grounds, no photos, claiming that she was writing an article on the heartfelt responsibility that the caretakers had taken upon themselves. Potter's Field management took the bait and agreed.

There are no headstones or other identification in Potter's Field, just administrative markers that identify the locations of the mass graves, stacked in threes, two across and twenty-five coffins long. That absence of gravestones adds further gloom to the dark, foreboding mood on the island. The dead are everywhere but remain unseen, ghosts. Conversation is uttered in respectful whispers.

"Patricia, stay here. I won't be long. I may be a bit upset and you may hear me but don't worry. I'll be fine." She then handed Patricia an envelope. "What you'll find inside belongs to me," she said. "We'll talk about it when I get back."

Susan then walked over to the guard who appeared to be in charge and showed him her papers. He seemed to be expecting her and greeted Susan with the sincere enthusiasm one would reserve for his or her biographer. They slowly walked through an entrance and onto the vast fields before them as she politely listened to his talk on the history of the island and its benevolent mission. When they were a distance from the Gazebo she asked if it would be okay to walk around a bit by herself to get the feel of the grounds. "Sure," he replied, "as long as I can see you." The island is a good mile long and there are areas where he could lose sight of her. She agreed and began her slow search, first for the pimp she had killed. She never knew his name but could feel him there. She needed his forgiveness.

Only some burial lines might be barely visible by virtue of the color changes in the ground and grass above, newer lines perhaps raised a bit and greener, the older possibly scrubby and slightly sunken. Susan found the pimp several hundred yards from where the guard stood watching her. Maybe it was the pimp's spirit or some mystical thing she couldn't explain, maybe it was the electrical vibration in his DNA that she felt, but Susan could sense him resting in the ground beneath her. 'Good,' she thought.

Susan apologized to his spirit and asked for his understanding and compassion so she could lift the burden from what she had done those many years before. The way she saw it her mutilation was no justification for killing him. He had his cross to bear just as she did. She asked and waited for minutes while the guard watched wondering what she was up to. Then she felt the lightening as though a weight had been gently lifted from her shoulders and chest. She breathed deeply and was free of him. It was done. She thanked the former pimp's generous spirit and then went in search of her mother.

She didn't have to look far. Her mother and the pimp died within days of each other. She found her innocent spirit peacefully asleep further along the same burial line. It would be the first time Susan spoke with her mother's spirit since her awakening in the forests of the northwest more than twenty years earlier, before she was a Packard, or even a Stanich.

As she approached her resting place, Susan could feel her mother's warm love as though she were there with her, alive and well. She wished it weren't so but there too was the pain from her mother's brutal life, where survival in and of itself was deemed success. Susan came to assure her mother that her daughter is okay and so add some peace to her eternity. Her daughter had made it out, off the streets, and she wanted her mother to know that her life was now good. So she began talking in the theater of her mind. Her mother never answered Susan. The dead don't talk. That's ridiculous. The conversation was one-way with her mother's response a feeling thing within Susan's consciousness, assuming her mother's role as well as her own, playing both parts in waiting places in her head and heart. Daughter to mother begets a regression to childhood even in midlife. And so it was:

"Mom, mom, mom...look, I'm alive. And I have kids and I'm clean. Never touched another thing, don't even smoke like you wanted. You'd be proud of me. I want you to be proud of me. Ma......I know you tried so hard. I know you did. I came here to tell you, you were a good mother to me. You were. And it worked. Ma, Look at me. I went to college, can you believe it!"

Susan spoke with her mother of her children, their names and what each looked like, and what she told them about their grandmother, how much she wished they could have known her, how much she wished their grandmother could have known them. She shared Jack too. Her mother's experience with men consisted of beasts that walk. Susan made sure her mother knew that there are gentler men; she got one. Susan poured everything she wanted to tell her mother as though she were standing there; twenty years worth of missing her. And Susan tearfully told her how much she wished she could have seen her alive just one more time, just once.

Then she let her love for her dead mother overflow from her spirit. Susan Stanich's expression of such is voiced. She didn't sob weepy tears. Instead, she fell to the earth above her mother's grave clawing at the dirt, and from the depths of her being let go the blood curdling cry of an animal beyond pain. She loved her mother and missed her and shared her love and loss with the universe through that inhuman howl until there was nothing left. That's how Susan Stanich prays. Whatever Gods there are, they heard. Even the shore birds stopped their skittering and listened. When she was done she stood up, still trembling a bit. After a calming moment she gazed at the ground one last time and turned to walk away, but stopped and returned to tell her mother one more thing.

"I have to tell someone and you're the only one. Ma, I think I'm a witch. I don't know how it works but this is wild." Susan and her mother laughed. They couldn't help themselves. Then Susan walked away.

When the guard saw her fall to the ground screaming he began running towards her. Halfway there she ceased her piercing cry and the guard stopped where he was. They met in the middle. He was about to let into her for disturbing the island but saw something in her eyes that convinced him it would be best not to say anything. They walked back together in silence. The tour was over.

Susan did eventually write the article. She is incapable of deception though on occasion she might sidestep, clam up or return an inquiry with an irrelevant comeback to get off some hook.

Patricia, along with everyone else on the island also heard her mother's wailing scream. The deaf would've felt it. When she walked through the entrance the other visitors stepped aside giving her plenty of space. "What are you trying to do to me?" her daughter asked as Susan approached.

"I had something to say to my mother. Mind your own business." And that was that, almost.

"Whose birth certificate is this?" asked her daughter.

"Oh, that. Mine. The afternoon is all yours."

"The birth certificate, Mom...who is Sandra DeSantos?"

"I was. We'll talk about it later. Let's go to the Empire State building. I heard the view at the top is something."

"Mom," Patricia said, "Who are you?"

"What would be more like it."

This was the first time Susan had taken their daughter along on one of her jaunts, giving Jack a rare, guiltless opportunity to do whatever he wanted. This was also the first time he and his wife would be apart for more than one night. Though he missed her when the lights went out, her absence allowed him to focus his energies on something other than his wife without distraction. Jack was very attracted to Susan, very. He loves her.

So, taking advantage of the opportunity, Jack and Max Stanich went on a fishing trip of great consequence. The mission was significant because their quarry was grayling, the rarest of trout-like fishes in the salmon family, still native in only two or three places in the lower forty-eight states. Max couldn't understand what the big deal was but his father was excited and intent so patient, gentle Max managed some enthusiasm to keep him company, and in the days ahead would allow his father to teach him how to fly fish, once again. The Stanich men flew into West Yellowstone to begin their quest for the elusive grayling about the same time Susan and Patricia were leaving Potter's Field. While they were fishing Susan went hunting. Returning to New York was the way she went about it.

The audition notice said nothing about the kidnapping that was to take place. When Alice Summers stepped through the door of the outer room where the auditions were being held she didn't know it but she already had the part. It was no coincidence that she fit the description of the role to a tee as though the part were written for her.

This wasn't her first cattle call. Inside the room were another half dozen or so aspiring actors, some sitting, some standing, all nervous. One of the actors pointed out an end table with a notepad on top. Alice walked over and saw that her name was on a call list along with an assigned number. There were about 20 other names, also with numbers. Her number was the highest, last. She knew the routine and sat, waiting her turn, watching each of the others go in a door and then come out until she was the only one left in the waiting room.

"He said you should go in," said the last actor as she walked out from the audition past Alice and left the building. Alice stood, flipped her hair in place and walked into what appeared to be a recording studio. She turned off her cell phone and left it in a box inside the entrance as a sign requested. Above the sunken floor was a dark, glassed-in booth. She could barely make out the figure of a man walking around inside. His voice came from speakers set all around the room. He was expecting her.

"Hi Alice. I'm glad you could make it today. You're a very pretty young lady and quite the actress I'm told."

"Thank you. I'm a little nervous."

"I promise you'll get over that. What we're going to do today is play with a monologue from a new comedy. The monologue is delivered between bites of a delicious chocolate cupcake. Do you think you can handle that?"

"I am hungry."

"Perfect."

An hour later, just after dusk, a car pulled up to the rear entrance of the small office complex where the studio was located. The man opened the rear door of the car and then walked into the building. Two minutes later he walked out steering Alice Summers into the back seat, and drove away. Just like that.

Alice Summers slept the hour's drive to the house the kidnapper had recently rented. The man completed applications for several other similar locations during the prior months. Each offered a finished basement and fit his need for a relatively isolated location. Over the past eight years he'd filed necessary paperwork anonymously by snail mail and courier services. Required deposits were made with cash and money orders. Rural landlords didn't employ background checks as often as urban property-owners. If the landlord or managing agent insisted on face time or requested too much information he forfeited the deposit and disappeared. The home owners happily kept the deposit and their mouth shut; slippage. The lease on the house he now inhabited was sealed with a money order covering a fat deposit and security, more than satisfying the landlord two states away.

As they approached the driveway an electric garage door opened. He drove into the garage and the door closed behind them.

Patricia expected the guided tour that her mother had promised would include Wall Street, Radio City and the Statue of Liberty, like normal people. She should've known better when her mother told her they had a big night ahead and insisted they take a nap at 7:00 PM. At 3:00 AM the following morning Susan pushed Patricia into a cab and slid in beside her.

"Take Broadway up to Washington Heights," she told the driver. "We'll be coming back the same way." The cabbie smiled. He'd lucked out with a fat roundtrip fare near the end of his shift.

As soon as she stepped in the cab Patricia became an instant New Yorker, which added child-like wonder to her delight at being chauffeured. The legend of colorful, entertaining New York taxi drivers had made an easy trip across the country, all the way to the northwest and landed in her imagination. She loved riding in a cab and acted like she and the cabbie were long lost friends, questioning him about how long he drove, where he came from, did he like driving a cab, had he met famous people. He answered her questions with "uh huh" and "sure." That's because his passable English couldn't keep up with her rapid fire queries. He had no idea what she was saying. Patricia suspected that might be the case but treated him like a celebrity anyway because the interchange gave her permission to assume the attitude of a New York sophisticate, kind of like riding a subway for the first time means you can then write a book about Brooklyn and back it up with real, on-the-ground experience. This desire to be part of the New York scene feeds the transition for hopeful wannabes like Patricia. Susan thought she was delightful and laid on some Bronx accent for the rest of the ride to make Patricia's transformation more authentic.

The bright lights of mid-town hotels and the theater district retreated behind them as the cab wended its way towards upper Manhattan where lifelong locals dwelled in often murky apartments behind triple locked doors. In the middle of the night few people are out and those who are about are often up to no good. Gone are the elegantly dressed tourists and business people. The hustle bustle of high energy activity gives way to just hustle. It's danger time. Susan Stanich was in her element.

"Drive slow," Susan said to the cabby as she was getting her bearings on Broadway in the Heights. Then, "Make a left at the next corner." Midway down the dark block she told him to pull over and stop.

"I'll be back in a few minutes," she said.

"Mom, where are you going...are you sure this is safe?"

"Don't get out of the car." And that was that.

Susan Stanich remembered. Many years had passed since she was there but she knew well the apartment house where she killed the pimp. She wasn't Susan Stanich then, or Packard. She was Knife, the nickname she'd earned as a hooker with a short temper. She peeked through one of the small windows of the outer door. Yeah, this was it she thought; same grubby inner door and the same single bulb lighting the vestibule. Old New York neighborhoods are fixed in time. She could see the corner where she lay in wait that night for the man who had mutilated her. This was where her old life ended and the extraordinary journey she'd embarked upon decades before had begun. She needed to walk that path again to gather about her whatever good will she could for the task ahead, which up to that time was stopping a possible psychotic with Narcissistic Personality Disorder and a penchant for impregnating the young. He would turn out to be little more than a warm-up.

This time her prayer was silent; it was for the pimp. Like many of us he was driven by influences beyond his inherent nature, pre-ordained by virtue of where he was born and into which family. Temperament plays a part but under the right guidance even the most aggressive personality can usually be channeled to a productive, beneficial life, though there may be exceptions. Perhaps some are born a beast. Susan didn't know how he came to be what he was but she certainly wasn't in any position to be his judge. So she forgave him as he had forgiven her and asked the forces about to let him rest in peace and then, not waiting for an answer, left. The prayer wasn't for her.

"How do you feel about taking a little ride to The Bronx," Susan asked the cabbie. "You can bring us back where you found us?" She spoke slowly and clearly and he got it.

"The Bronx? Now we're going to The Bronx?" said Patricia

"You said you wanted to see New York. It's only 4. The night is young." Then to the driver, "Well, whattaya say?"

"I have to call dispatch and see if I can keep the cab for an extra hour or two." He didn't say it quite that well but that was what he meant. Drivers' lease for the shift ended at 5:00am though on occasion they made an exception if it wasn't a regular thing. He made the call, then turned around and gave Susan a big smile in broken English. Now he was an even happier cabbie.

Halfway to The Bronx Patricia's smart mouth opened the door to her mother's past: "Okay Sandra, let's have it. Who are you?"

Susan carefully weighed her response as every parent should when addressing issues that will impact the lives of their children. That responsibility encompasses virtually every moment until their offspring fly on their own and sometimes long beyond that. Our breath is their breath; our words become their thoughts and actions and shape the life before them.

So she began: "Patricia, beneath the world you know there is another, an invisible dark place that's right there in front of your eyes but you never really see it. I was part of that other world. I am Sandra DeSantos. I am still her. She is within me. Being here now, she's closer to the surface than I care. There are places Patricia that are jungle. Humans become worse than animals doing terrible things to one another to survive, the ones who live. I knew many who didn't. But I survived as a prostitute. There's nothing about life on the streets that you should regard as necessary, noble or courageous. There is no romantic bravado that deserves admiration. These are the ugly acts of desperate people. That I am here with you...think dumb luck Patricia. Maybe it had to do with my genes. More likely I was fortunate not to have walked down the wrong street. Luck Patricia. That's what I think grace is, a stroke of luck. I did nothing to earn who I am today. Just luck.

"When I was your age something terrible happened in that building where we stopped. I'm never going to tell you anymore about it than I already have; guess what you want but you mustn't ever ask.

"Patricia, I won't let you walk in my shoes. Never happen. You should know how my path began and who I am because I am in you. This is who we were once. That's over. You never have to suffer as I did to live an extraordinary life, a creative life if that's what you want. There are no dues to pay. That's nonsense. You don't need the motivation of painful experience to excel in anything. You simply need the joy of doing. That'll work fine. Got it?"

"What's in The Bronx?"

"My old neighborhood where I grew up. I want to say something to my dead father and we'll be done."

"What are you going to say?"

"Well, you should know...my father was a brute, sadistic, an alcoholic. He raped me when I was eight. I guess you could say I was insane for many years after: Prostitution is how I punished myself for being damaged goods. I want him to know that I forgive him. He had his devils. He wasn't born an animal."

"Mom...."

"Patricia, you wanted to know, now listen...he was the product of his environment just like the pimp, and me. But I got lucky. They didn't. Forgiving him is for me. It will help free me from what's left of my anger. I need it. He can do with it what he wants. I don't care. That much of a saint, I'm not."

"Okay, mom, okay. Does Dad know all this?"

"Some of it. He doesn't ask and I don't volunteer. Why burden him. With you it's different."

"Why?"

"You're the daughter. Who better?"

"After this are we done?"

"With this part, yes."

"Then we have three days left before going home. What would you like to do?"

"Oh, what would I like to do? Well, that's a first. I'd like us to rent a car."

"Where are we going?"

"Home. We're driving back across the country so you can count the stars with me."

Half an hour later they were double parked in front of an apartment house in the south Bronx. Susan got out of the car and walked to the front of the building and stood in the pre-dawn light looking up at a set of darkened windows on the second floor. Her daughter could see her animated talking and gesturing with her hands, sometimes with her fists. After ten minutes she stopped and dropped to her knees and held out her hands, palms up.

A moment or two later Susan stood, put herself together and walked back to the cab. “I asked my father to let go of me. He needs some time but I think he will.”

“You’re something lady,” said the happy cabbie as he headed back to the city.

Chapter 4

Two days after Alice Summers was taken, her profile was flagged on Lou Pasquale's missing persons report, the fifth that came across his desk that morning. He made his routine call to the parents to cull a possible kidnapping from a more likely runaway but was stopped before he got the first question out of his mouth.

"He called us last night," the hysterical mother of Alice Summers screamed at him. "He said she won't be harmed, she'll be back home in seven or eight months. What is he talking about? What is going on? Where is she? What are the police doing?"

In the instant Pasquale knew he didn't need intuition or a hunch to conclude this was probably their kidnapper. "We're on it ma'am. I'm in charge of a division devoted to finding your daughter."

"Where is she? Is she safe? What's going on?"

"We're doing everything possible to locate her. Ma'am, I know you've spoken with some of our officers yesterday but if it's all right with you I'd like to speak with you. Can I and another detective come to see you this afternoon?"

"Now, right now, I want to talk to someone now."

"Our office is several hours away. We'll be there as soon as possible."

"Please hurry, please."

"Yes, ma'am. We should be there by mid-afternoon. In the meantime other members of our unit and local detectives in your precinct are doing everything possible to find Alice. Ma'am, we don't think she's in any danger."

"You don't, hah? How the hell do you know?"

"Well, please take my word on it. He's not going to hurt her. I'm sure."

"You can't promise me that can you?"

"No, I can't. But I'd bet on it. We'll see you in a few hours."

Pasquale hadn't known about the call. That changed things. If it was the kidnapper and Pasquale was certain it was, he was getting bolder, arrogant, tormenting the parents and blatantly thumbing his nose at the police. It was also possible that in his twisted mind he thought he was reassuring the parents. Millman was sitting across from him and could see from Pasquale's side of the conversation and his partner's demeanor that another kidnapping had occurred.

"Damm," said Lou, "I hate surprises. He called her up. Can you believe that? Why weren't we told about that call?" He wondered if the parents of the other girls had also received a call from the kidnapper. "Get your coat. We're going for a ride. I really wish that Stanich or Packard woman or whoever she is was here."

Jack Stanich also wished his wife were nearby to help soothe his delicate ego. Inside every father and son fishing team are competing boys dying to brag about the fish they catch. Alas, Jack was left with no reason to boast. He hadn't managed the capture of the rare grayling he'd prophesized by virtue of his natural instincts and keen senses. Quite a few decent cutthroat and rainbow trout managed to find their way on the Stanich hooks, but they didn't count, not this trip. Had Jack kept his mouth shut and not been specific regarding the grayling they sought he would have been able to maintain hero status in his son's eyes. He screwed that up with grayling promises he couldn't keep. Now, without Susan he was alone in pumping himself back up. He always missed her as soon as she was out of sight and usually felt compelled to rationalize a reason for needing her closer. He really was lost without her. Yes, that good.

In desperation, the fishermen did Hidden Lake on their last day, as close to fishing in a barrel as one can get, a hike-in hideaway that proved to the Stanich men that there are big fat trophy trout just waiting to torment them. All they had to do to find them was look in the water. Though not grayling, the huge rainbows were all over the place. Regrettably, the fish liked where they were because neither Jack nor Max managed to entice any to rise to their fly and join them for a photo session. The fish, probably laughing, decided they would rather swim in front of the Stanich men barely a few feet away. They were close enough to grab with the hands and put on the hook, which occurred to Max.

Typically, mellow Max couldn't care less what they caught but, as usual, pretended he did by delivering a very visible sharing of the grayling setback, and followed that up with trophy trout disappointment anguish. He also offered generous contributions to the analysis of their bad luck. Together, they came up with: wrong air or water temperature – the grayling were spawning, were about to spawn or had just spawned – the sun was out or it was in. Jack even suggested that the trophy trout just ate because he was hungry; anthropomorphic reasoning. Max found his dad's frustration very entertaining, well worth the trip.

And Jack enjoyed his son's efforts at compassion. Max was just like his father only slightly shorter. A growth spurt in his twelfth year put him within several inches of his father's 6'2". It would be several years before Max began the rebellion against parental oversight that is necessary in order to attain one's majority as an independent adult. Accordingly, his parents treasured these last years when he would still be their little boy regardless of his height, even if he was quite tall for adorable.

When Patricia called her father to inform him they were driving cross country and wouldn't be back for a week Jack was not a happy man; first no grayling and now no Susan. Max understood.

Once the kidnapper made the call to the Summers residence the possibility of Alice's disappearance being a runaway went out the window. In the kidnapper's previous abductions sometimes a month went by before the police reacted. The call changed everything, fast. By the time Pasquale and Miller showed up Alice's mother had provided photos of her daughter to the county sheriff's office, which were then passed out at a press conference to local newspapers and TV stations. An amber alert had been posted statewide as well as announced on the media of adjoining states. Alice's picture was all over social media. Her mother's earlier hysteria turned within as her mind settled onto nightmare scenarios of the worst possible outcomes. The detectives found her sitting on a living room couch with a fixed gaze, handkerchief in hand, dabbing at the tears continually streaming down her cheeks.

Pasquale gently sat next to her. “Mrs. Miller, I’m Lou Pasquale, the detective you spoke with a few hours ago. I know this is a terrible ordeal but it’s important that we speak. Can I have a few minutes of your time?”

It took the woman a moment to bring herself back from her inward spiral. Swollen red eyes slowly turned towards Pasquale. When she spoke she was barely audible: “I’m worried. Alice is very forthright, sometimes too much so. I’m afraid she may say something to anger whoever took her. She doesn’t think before she speaks.”

“He won’t harm her, like he said when he called. We believe him.”

“Why should I believe him, or you? He kidnapped her. His mind isn’t right.”

“Mrs. Miller, there are things we think you should know. Some of what we’re going to tell you will put your mind to rest, some may disturb you, but I want to assure you that whoever he is, he won’t harm her. We’re confident your daughter will be returned to you safe and sound.”

“You don’t know that.”

“He’s done this before Mrs. Miller. All the others came back home healthy and happy.”

“The others? What others?”

“This man has kidnapped a number of girls before?”

“And they came back home? And they were okay?”

“Yes, ma’am.”

“Why does he do this?”

“When they come home, they’re pregnant.”

As terrified as Mrs. Miller was she couldn’t help but let a slight smile appear at the corners of her mouth. “You’re a nice fellow detective. My Alice won’t be coming back pregnant. You don't know her, neither does he. I just hope she comes home soon and keeps her mouth shut."

On the third day of Alice Summers's captivity she met the kidnapper for the first time. When he unlocked the only exit door her heart began fluttering and her knees went weak, an uncontrollable shiver rippled through her body. He walked in masked, carrying a food tray, locking the door behind him. She stood motionless, trembling and scared. Until then meals were slipped through a bottom slot in the exit door that was in the largest of the three rooms. She had eaten nothing and pushed the food back each time it came through the opening, paranoid about being poisoned and glad she was too terrified to eat. Hunger was the least of her concerns.

Alice thought she was in an apartment, one without windows, which she found odd but was too disoriented to realize it was a finished basement. For the first day she did a lot of yelling and cursing, which got her nothing except a hoarse throat.

The main room was quite large, which seemed to Alice to have been designed as a family room, with a ping pong table at one end and a large screen TV at the other. A long horseshoe shaped sofa of rich, worn leather faced the TV. Two matching, opposing easy-chairs were nestled against either end of the sofa facing one another. A finely finished cherrywood bookcase was loaded with CDs and DVDs. Remotes had been placed where she could easily find them. The other two rooms consisted of bedroom and kitchen/dining area. The refrigerator had been well stocked, as was the freezer. Cabinets above the stove contained a variety of nuts, soups and canned fruits and vegetables, all untouched by Alice. The bedroom was adequate, clean and practical. She wouldn't sleep on the bed. That was too permanent, a sign of resignation she wouldn't permit. So she slept on the couch, fully clothed and ready to run. But she did use the shower and on the second day wore the fresh clothes that had been waiting for her on the bed. They fit. The decor in the three rooms was tasteful, the walls generously finished in lush red oak, trimmed in dark mahogany. Under different circumstances the space would have been quite comfortable, even warm.

She'd spent the latter part of the first two days watching news coverage of her kidnapping, when she wasn't crying or yelling. By the third day she was done crying and replaced her fear with anger. She was really pissed off. She figured the understudy in the upcoming school production of "All's Well That Ends Well" would be getting her applause and that didn't sit well with her. Even under the circumstance her ambition was like a competitive rock. She had set her sights on stardom when she was barely eight and a kidnapping was a diversion she didn't appreciate.

"Good afternoon," said the kidnapper.

"Fuck you," said Alice. "How the fuck am I supposed to know it's afternoon? There isn't a window in this prison. Fuck you."

"I'm not going to hurt you, not ever."

"Are you crazy? You kidnapped me. My parents must be out of their minds worrying what happened to me."

"I called them to assure them you'll be fine."

"Oh, great. You kidnap me and call my parents to tell them I'm fine? You're a fucking nut, you know that. Take off that stupid mask. You look like a jerk."

Alice Summers was not what the kidnapper expected. Though obviously frightened, that didn't stop her from confronting him. Then again he'd never before had to deal with an ambitious, aspiring actress hell bent on stardom. He had to concede that this time he might be dealing with more than a handful of quirky attitude. And this was only the beginning. So he tried a slightly direct, fatherly approach.

"You have a mouth like a garbage pail," he said.

"Fuck, fuck, fuck...how's that. What do you think I am, you're fucking doily? You're crazy. This is so not fun."

"I'll never hurt you. I promise, never, no matter what. I couldn't. It's not in my nature. It may appear that I'm keeping you secured for now, but that will soon change and you'll be able to come and go as you please."

"Secured? Secured? What the fuck does that mean? Secured from what, who, you? Let me be insecure and get me the fuck out of here and back into the dangerous world. Let's do that. Secured? You are one fucking nut. You'll never hurt me? How about we kick you in the balls and test it. Nut....Secured...."

"You will be going back to your parents safe and sound. I promise. But I'm not so sure you'll want to. I know all this sounds strange now but if you give it some time I think you'll discover that I'm right. We're going to make a beautiful baby, you and I."

"A baby? A baby? You are crazy. I want to go home now, you fucking nutjob."

"Soon you'll feel differently. I would appreciate it if you didn't use that kind of language. It really isn't very becoming to a beautiful young woman."

"Fuck you asshole. Motherfucker."

Kidnapper, meet Alice Summers.

At the same time that the Stanich men were dining on fish & chips to lift Jack's bruised spirit, the Stanich women were driving through a beautiful Ohio night. Since arriving in New York, Susan's sleeping pattern had changed, much to the exhaustion of her daughter. It seemed that her mother slept during the day and was wide awake and rearing to go around dusk. And she was right. Susan's younger self Knife had taken over part of her being and had been busy as Susan slept till mid-day or the late afternoon. The hour they went to sleep or woke up had become kind of random, but deep in the night they drove. Patricia was getting worn out while her mother was becoming more energized. Somewhere in the middle of the state Susan decided it was time to share what she could with her daughter.

"Patricia, have you ever noticed how lights go out when I'm around?"

"Yeah. And. So what? They go out all the time."

"Don't you think that's a little weird?"

"Nope, but the way you know when the phone's going to ring is out there. You do lots of stuff like that. What I'd like to know is what's with the no electric thing. Why are we the only people I know without a TV? And you have a computer."

"It's not for entertainment and it's not for using."

"Mom, you're different. I know that. We all do. We talk about you sometimes, Dad and I. Max doesn't pay attention like that but he loves the funny stuff you do with people, the weirder the better. What are you trying to tell me? Is this going to be worse than the prostitute thing?"

"You'll live."

"Oh, no."

"Shut-up...terrible things occurred the last days I was in New York, but something also starting happening to me, inside of me, inside my head. I was driven insane or sane. I don't which but there was more of me. I don't know how else to describe it. There was more of me and more of the world around me. It started slowly and then got bigger and bigger very fast."

"More of what?"

"Me. Everything. Deeper, brighter, wider, clearer, my brain, the way it worked. I started knowing things that I couldn't possibly have known, like someone was pouring information into the top of my head. I didn't just see people. I saw who they were, their history, why they looked the way they did. I was changed. I still am. If you think lights go out now, you should've seen them popping then. Electricity doesn't do well around me and too much stings my skin. That's why we don't have television and other electric stuff. Half the time they won't work anyway, like with the lights. The battery in the computer doesn't bother me and it runs, maybe because it's not alternating current. That's why we recharge everything in the garage."

"That's the only outlet. We never use the car."

"We do sometimes, when it's necessary; the less the better. Patricia, every thought has electricity, a vibration maybe, something like that. Everything we say or do too. Somehow we transmit our actions and thinking out into the universe. None of the energy disappears, an Einstein thing. All the thoughts of all the creatures that ever existed are still out there swirling around. It falls on us constantly, but maybe our brain isn't developed enough to sense it. Maybe what happened to me made me sensitive to that energy. It doesn't come to me in words or thoughts. Things just kind of appear in my head like dreams. Electricity blocks it.

"I have no idea what happened to me or why. There's lots more but I don't think it would be wise for me to expose you to things I can't explain. Patricia I tell you this because the more you know the less likely that anything can happen that would put you in danger. One kidnapping is enough for this life. Keep these things to yourself. Our profile has to be low. That detective already suspects too much."

"Can what happened to you happen to me?"

"I doubt it. It's probably not hereditary," she told her daughter. "I don't think anyone is born this way. You are not me in that way and likely never will be for reasons I don't understand. What I want to know is how you knew I would cooperate with the cops and come to New York?"

"I figured it out. You were with them too long. If you had refused to cooperate you would've been out of there in less than a minute. So I knew you were going to help them. And you've been talking about New York a lot lately. The trip back here was an educated guess. I'm smart."

"A wiseass is more like it."

"Yep, that's me. It's inherited."

"Moron."

"I like wiseass better. While we're at it, do you really drive molesters crazy? Why do they think you fly?"

Susan burst out laughing and couldn't stop, and it was Stanich contagious. Patricia joined her in uncontrollable giggles. As soon as it died down they made the mistake of peeking at each other and the laughing started all over, repeatedly until they were drained, holding their cheeks to stop the smirk that by then was hurting.

"Oh, God, that was good," said Susan when she was sure they were done.

"Mom, I think Max is keeping a diary of all the stuff you do."

"I'll kill that kid."

"I want to watch. So, let's have it...what's with the perverts?"

"I find deviants who hurt children."

"You what?"

"I track them down, sometimes through the internet. When I find them I have fun with them. I scare the shit out of them. That's where I go when I disappear once in a while. I keep doing it until they turn themselves in to the police to get away from me."

"One of them will hurt you. You have to stop."

"They can't hurt me. And you know enough to play amateur psychiatrist and guess my motivation. I'm very sensitive to the energy of bad people. It sticks to me. I can feel evil in the air like I'm attuned to it. It's the energy I was talking about. The best way I can describe it is that I can smell a molester, an abuser. Their scent isn't clean and I can feel the bad energy, their guilt. They're always scared. Fear gives off a very distinct aura, feeling, like their brains operate on a different frequency. Something similar happens with their victims. I can feel their pain, damage. It floats to me. It's everywhere. I often find it difficult to separate the sources. But when I can zero in on one of them I scare the shit out of them. It's fun. But I don't fly through the air. That's absurd. Patricia, it's all in their minds. The only time you'll see my feet leave the ground is in jump rope." This was true, for the most part. Her feet never really move. And like she said, it's all in their minds.

"Are you a witch?"

"Patricia, you still believe in Santa Claus, don't you?"

"Mom!"

"Enough foolish questions. Let's look at stars tonight." There, a perfect example of how Susan Stanich avoided lying when necessary, an exceptional side-stepper.

They drove through the late night for several more hours quietly taking in the dark, soothed by the steady hum of the car's engine. Near the Illinois border Susan pulled the car off at a rest area and retrieved a blanket from the backseat. She spread it on the ground in a picnic area off to the side of the parking and away from the glare of a welcome center. Far from the light pollution of the nearest city, the heavens were clear. The two of them lay down to watch the stars just as a shooting star streaked across the sky welcoming them to Knife's night.

"Watch the stars closely," said Susan. "Can you see their colors? Pick one near the horizon that has color. You'll see the color will change making the star dance blues, reds and yellows. The atoms and particles that create the dance are made up of thoughts pouring from the universe and flowing through the light. It's all about energy Patricia."

Chapter 5

Half a day earlier the Stanich women had just gone to sleep at 7:00 am. Two thousand miles to the west it was still dark before the first light of dawn on the outskirts of Portland, Oregon. A peeping Tom was cruising a familiar route, one where he'd spotted a partially open window shade on the side of a house weeks before. The window was barely visible, facing a row of trees and mostly hidden from the street side, a perfect scenario for peeping. If he looked carefully as he drove past it was possible to catch a view of part of the room. One morning he was rewarded when he caught a fleeting glimpse of a naked girl. He then made the route his only routine.

He'd spotted her a number of times since. As he slowly drove past that early morning he could see that the girl was up and going about her daily regimen, one that after weeks of watching he imagined he knew by heart. But it was all in his mind as was most of his existence outside of peeping. She'd get up and turn on the lights. After getting her breakfast she would return to her bedroom and close the door to the rest of the house. He could picture her, still wearing pajamas, entering the bathroom, closing the door and taking her shower. When she came out of the bathroom she would have a towel around her. Then she would remove the towel and wrap it around her hair, leaving her naked. The girl would then dress. That morning the man's compulsion peaked and overcame his fear of getting caught. He could no longer control himself. He knew he would have only a few moments to catch her undressed if he could get to the window in time.

He quickly drove his car around the corner and parked on a busier street near stores so as to hide in morning activity. Flushed, he walked back towards the house as fast as he could without attracting attention. When he got closer he slowed his steps, bottling his urgency even as his breathing became deeper and faster driven by the pulse of obsession. His eyes were in back of his head and on both sides seeking any activity from nearby houses. Even a distant dog barking would have spooked him and had him continue walking past the house to try another day. But there was only silence. He turned into the side of the house and casually walked towards the window. He would find a surprise there waiting to greet him.

Deep in Susan's sleep the witch Knife could smell the peeper at the window. That's where the witch found him. He never saw her coming. Suddenly she was there at his side."Hi Ronny," she whispered. The peeper sucked in his breath and stopped breathing entirely, stuck in panic. "Don't move a muscle," she added, softly, almost soothingly so as not to alarm the occupants or upset the peeper any more than he already was. "And don't say a word. We don't want to disturb anyone now do we? Come." She walked him out onto the sidewalk. "Ronny, I know you. I even know your license plate and where you live. I know everything about you. You're going to the police to join the ranks on the sex offender list. It's free. If you don't I'll bring them to you and it's jail, baby, jail. And if I ever catch you doing this again, same thing, jail. For all you know my last peeper got a year but only lasted a few months, if you know what I mean. Got it, you fucking scumbag piece of shit?"

Across the street a house light went on. Ronny the peeper glanced over and then back to Susan. And she was gone, vanished. He began crying. They always cried like a baby when she was through with them. That's because they were stuck in some bad turn on the road of their early childhood; they've been crying ever since. Susan felt sincere compassion for their pain but they had to be stopped just the same. An hour later Ronny the peeper was in a police station. He couldn't wait to get there. The way he figured it, he'd had a vision. God was after him.

The girl had no idea anything had taken place outside her bedroom window but for the first time it occurred to her that maybe it would be a good idea to lower the shades completely down. One never knows.

The witch Knife smiled in Susan's sleep.

When Stanley Millman picked up the call at the start of their shift early the following morning Pasquale closely watched him as always to gauge the importance of their next case. "Well, what do we have?"

"A self-confessed peeper. This time in Portland."

"No."

"Yes. And I have more bad news for you. He ID'd the photo of the Stanich woman we e-mailed, says she convinced him to stop peeping. He thinks she was an angel"

"Packard. Packard. For now on she's always Packard. She's at it again, It's her. I know it's her. Where's her cell number?"

Susan Stanich answered just as she and Patricia were about to go to sleep. It was 11:00am in the Illinois motel that accepted the extra $20 Susan offered to encourage them to stray from their posted sign in/sign out times. A 25% occupancy rate said 'Sure, why not.'

"Mrs. Stanich?" was all he got out and she hung up. Pasquale called again. This time Patricia answered. "My mother doesn't want to talk to you. She says she'll see you when we get back."

"Get back from where? You're here."

"No we're not. Hey, Mom, where are we?" Pasquale could hear Susan's answer in the background. "Moms says she thinks we're in Illinois."

"Illinois? What are you doing in Illinois?" The girl cupped the phone so he could barely hear a brief, muffled conversation.

"We're sightseeing. Mom wants to know if you want us to bring back souvenirs?"

"No thank you," he replied. And the girl hung up. "Jesus Christ that woman's going to give me a heart attack."

"Maybe she is a witch."

"Why do you say stupid things like that?"

"You're the one who talks to babies about the weather."

Chapter 6

Sandra DeSantos aka Knife/Susan Stanich/Susan Packard, and then Susan Stanich again, continued her passage back in time, back to when she was blessed with a state of grace, when she became aware and starting seeing the face of the forces about in every smile, leaf and puppy. Reliving her earlier life where the awakening began was the purpose of her return to New York. Revisiting those she left behind was the quickening. So she returned to the origin of the forces that favored her to bring them back into her fold in full. It worked before.

Regardless of the rationalization with which the serial kidnapper managed to delude himself, he was a destructive, delusional man depriving innocents of their childhood and destroying families. But she couldn't smell him, couldn't even feel his victims. There was no fear or anger that she could sense. This was different, which is why she needed to gather about her all of her powers to find him, stop him. But in the end even that wouldn't work because her aim was off. He wasn't the reason she was being drawn back to her origins. But she didn't know that yet.

When still a child, Susan escaped New York and bused her way to the northwest. While in the city with Patricia she was too overwhelmed by racing emotions to allow the quiet mind required for contemplation. The leisurely pace of the cross-country drive, removed from chores and responsibilities, gave her space for the reflection she sought. As she retraced the original journey of her initiation into the mysteries of the hidden world, each revelatory milestone of that extraordinary journey would come back to her fresh. Her mind would expand.

Patricia wasn't a child that demanded attention and knew her mother wanted to be left alone. She herself needed breathing room to absorb as best she could the secrets her mother had entrusted to her. They drove together in their own good company and the tranquility each needed.

Sandra DeSantos was only twelve years old and dangerously wild as are those who don't care whether they live or die. With the cards she was dealt she figured death couldn't be any worse than her life. The only good thing that happened as far back as she could remember was the day her father died the previous year, the happiest day of her life. Biological history was the sole basis for their connection; there was no relationship. He was the first man who used her for sex, from the time she was barely eight. He would drink into an incoherent stupor, then take what he wanted because she was there. And she despised her mother because she was unable to stop him. At twelve she punished her mother and herself by making men pay for sex. Tall for her age and wearing makeup she could pass for eighteen, though some of the men she serviced had to suspect she was underage. So what.

The young prostitute Sandra DeSantos began carrying a knife after she had been badly beaten in an alley in the financial district by two high-end drunks. During the day the men were respected traders. In the middle of the night, after several rounds of boilermakers, they became a conscienceless duo of brutes that tag-teamed their aggressive natures on any hooker impressed by the wads of money they flashed. They were rough trade, too rough for the girl. Brought to her knees by an iron grip on her hair, she punched the one in the balls and tried to run but was tripped by the other. By the time they were done teaching her a lesson she had several broken ribs. She never again walked into the night without a folded barber's razor that she wouldn't hesitate to employ with the slightest provocation. By the age of thirteen Sandra DeSantos had gained a reputation and a nickname: Knife. Though there was a drug-induced craziness surrounding many of the street hookers, her complete indifference to life and death placed her in a category by herself, a rationally feared and respected competitor cruising the avenues of Manhattan. When she staked out a street the other hookers walked. To this day she never steps into the world without that knife.

Sandra DeSantos was born with her independent streak, wasn't part of any pimp's stable, which was bad for the rules of the business and could prove dangerously infectious. Pimps knew of the girl but were unable to catch up with her until an unlucky night in her sixteenth year that left her with a badly broken nose and deep lacerations on her breasts. Two weeks later her mother died and she went crazy.

The accumulation of horrors from those events instigated the journey that would favor her with grace. She started her journey by blackmailing a dozen former well-heeled tricks, changed her name to Susan Stanich and Sandra DeSantos was no more, and got on a bus. But our history never leaves us, rather it rolls around in our minds getting smaller and smaller, and deeper and deeper. She would always be Knife, part of her living on the edge.

"Telepathy, let's talk about telepathy," Susan said somewhere in Iowa, breaking the quiet that had comfortably settled on the two travelers

"Please, no more electricity?" said Patricia.

"It's very interesting. Don't you ever think about how telepathy finds its way?"

"Never. No one thinks about that, but I want to know why you changed your name."

"I didn't like the other one."

"Mom."

"My mother dying, school records...I was afraid someone would come looking and I'd end up in an institution. Besides there was nothing left for Sandra DeSantos." She didn't mention that the pimp had friends. But she was done with that conversation. "Here's what I think," she continued. "We each operate on a unique frequency. I bet it's coded into our DNA. Yeah, that's how it works, like our fingerprints or better yet the IP address on a computer. "

"Are you having a good time with yourself?"

"Yeah, that's it. And then the frequency imprints with people we're around, we become connected, attuned, like their frequency becomes embedded in our memory cache, the way we remember a face. It's in our RAM. Wow, I've been wondering about that. This has to be it. What do you think?"

"That can't be why you changed your name."

Alice Summers had the fear gene missing, which may have been why Susan would never feel her. The energy that sparks from fear and terror is a lightning storm that pierces

Susan, while the gently rolling seas of everyday life are little more than the undistinguishable calm of the universe. Alice was centered and confident right to her core. As Susan and Patricia were chatting somewhere in Iowa, Alice was laughing at the kidnapper and laughter goes right over Susan's head. No stop signs. Just the way it is.

The Seattle media were televising interviews with two of the kidnapper's previous victims, glowing young mothers recalling their seven-month adventure, proudly presenting their offspring, half siblings, to the world. Little more than children themselves, the mothers had the fixed beaming smiles of cult look-a-likes. The toddlers, eleven months apart, appeared normal. Their mothers were telling the interviewer why they had accepted the kidnapper's new-age name suggestions: Moonrise and Sunrise, a bit retro but the girls were too young to have known the 60's and thought the kidnapper very original, on the forefront of a trend they would spearhead.

"Hey kidnapper," Alice yelled at the exit door. "You gotta come see this. The dorks you knocked up have your kids on TV. They look just like you. They're wearing masks too. Better hurry." That, of course, was her idea of a joke, which snowballed into guffaws aimed at the door.

Then a video segment from one of Alice's school plays was aired for the entire world to see and she was stunned, swept away with pure joy. The possibilities of fast-tracking her route to fame a huge bulb that suddenly went off in her head . "Thank you, thank you, thank you," she yelled at the door.

The door opened and the man walked in to find Alice Summers overcome with gratitude. "You made me a star," she announced. "I'm famous now, all because of you. Other than the baby thing I'll do whatever you want. You're a genius. Keep me as long as you like."

The man walked across the room with his eye fixed on the TV but the news segment had moved on to the weather forecast. "What do they look like?" he asked, sincerely curious as any father might be who had never seen his child, their faces a blank, memory of them empty. Whatever she would tell him...that would be them. He joined Alice on the couch but far enough away so as not to make her uncomfortable. His MO was to never approach his victims in any way that could threaten them. Part of his seduction technique was to overcome them with boredom till there was nothing else to do. His library of DVDs included the mushiest of romantic tear jerkers to help nudge things along. And then there were his poetry readings. Alice would prefer boredom.

"You've never seen your children?"

"No." He was embarrassed by the admission, almost ashamed.

"Well, I can't say they look like their father because I have no idea what you look like. Take off the mask, let me see and I'll tell you."

"Alice, I have an I.Q. of almost 150. I'm not going to be so easily fooled. You'll have to come up with a better ploy, one that might work."

"Really? Trying to tell me what a great gene pool you have? You should have done your homework, idiot. I turned down Mensa when I was seven. You're dealing with 152 here. I'm not even sure you're worth talking to. And I'm certainly not going to dilute my eggs by stepping down a notch in your bed. But you did get me on TV so I'll cut you some slack and talk slow with little words. Don't you think your children need their father? Didn't you think about that?"

"Have you ever thought about having children?"

"Sure, but not with a moron like you. And not before I have a career. I can't have a kid now."

"Of course you could."

"No, I can't. I'm on the pill, idiot. When I'm not I become a hormonal monster that hates males. You'll see. When I have kids they'll have a father and live a normal life and they won't be named Stardust or some other name guaranteed to fuck them up. Why did you do that to those children?"

"There's no need to keep calling me names."

"I agree. What's your name?" He said nothing. "Okay, you're idiot."

"Why do you insist on being vulgar?"

"If it's good enough for Adele, it's good enough for me. She's great, voice like an angel, mouth like a truck driver. Fact is you're a first class fuck-up with low self esteem living out a very childish fantasy. I'm only a kid and I can see it. Me and Adele call it the way we see it...well, idiot, what are we going to do for the next seven months? Monopoly?"

"Where does someone like you come from?"

Janice Goldman was having almost as much fun as Alice.

Lou Pasquale wasn't himself. He really liked Janice and naturally was terrified as most men are when they come down with acute infatuation. If the fascination lasts we call it love and poetic misery blossoms. Contrary to common myth, status quo for the first blush of true love features jealousy, possessiveness and insecurity. Pasquale had all the symptoms. And Janice liked him, very much, but it wasn't in her reserved nature to let it be known beyond a wink and a smile. Poor Pasquale, he was so wretched that Janice decided she should marry him to keep him happy, a case of husband-at-first-sight. How to tell him without telegraphing her enthusiasm was the question. At the same time he was trying to figure out how to ask her.

Some may conclude their willingness to commit at such an early stage premature but neither of them saw it that way. Respect grows with time but that isn't the attraction that leads to the bedroom or the altar. Though they held off rushing into sex as they danced their way into their future together, they couldn't wait to get their hands on one another but pretended otherwise. It was as true as love can get.

That Lou was a detective and Janice a gynecologist didn't bother either of them, though it might make good literary sense to create some dramatic conflict regarding an income disparity that should plague the match. But that wasn't the case. He was too centered for such nonsense. Chemistry was the bond that would tie them regardless of their differences, a spiritual thing with a physical face. As far as he was concerned, the more money, the better. She felt the same way. They were adults.

Common interests are often overrated. That's why we have other people in our lives. What they had in common was what counted: Pasquale adored babies and Janice wanted some. They'd both get what they wished for. Fortunately it was the same thing. They complemented one another rather than overlap in spite of the odd pairing. And they looked good together. There are even stranger matches. After all Jack Stanich is a machinist, a tool and die maker, and Susan is a witch. And that turned out fine.

Janice Goldman, like Jack Stanich, has little to do with our story, yet she too makes a contribution when it's needed.

During their second date Janice gave Lou her take on the kidnapper. "He just wants to get laid and he likes teenagers because they don't intimidate him, very simple." She saw the kidnapping and role playing as utter rationalization, bullshit. "He's an immature, sequential polygamist on some delusional trip, nothing more."

"Janice," he said, "who cares about his motivation. He's a kidnapper." Men always use their love's first name a lot in the beginning so it'll become a habit and they won't screw up using the wrong name. If she hadn't meant a great deal to him she would've been honey or sweetheart.

"He knows he's going to get caught," she said.

"Why do you say that?"

"He wants to get caught. If you don't catch him, he'll start leaving big juicy clues. If that doesn't work he'll jump in your lap sooner or later."

"Why?"

"Because he'll want the world to know who he is. He's a nutjob with Narcissistic Personality Disorder."

"That's what she said."

"Who?"

Poor Jack. Had he and Max remained in West Yellowstone for a few more days they could have almost seen Susan and Patricia drive past on their way back home to Washington State. Knowing she was only one state away would have been comforting. Be that as it may, he and Max had spent the morning doing something, anything to keep his mind off her not being closer where he could protect her, his rationalization of the day. He and Max were now preparing homemade pizza for lunch to kill the afternoon. And then they would eat the mess. When Susan and Patricia were home they often made pizza for the family, and always had to eat it themselves as punishment for wasting food.

"Where do you think they are today?" asked Jack.

Max took a moment to answer and then said: "They're near Cheyenne, Wyoming at the Wild West Motel. Mom's sleeping. Patricia's calling us." Jack looked at Max in the way that was usually reserved for Patricia when they wrongly suspected she may have inherited Susan's peculiar nature.

Max was a quiet child. Always had been, not that he wasn't in the middle of every happening and activity. He just didn't talk much. When asked a question he wasn't one to respond quickly, rather thoughtfully. And he spoke in a measured fashion, slowly. He seemed to be an intelligent child and he was, as well as a prankster. Their concern about Patricia inheriting her mother's talents was misplaced. They were looking in the wrong place. This would be the day they found out.

"Right," said Jack, and then the phone rang. Jack kept looking at Max as he walked over to the phone and answered: "Hello." It was Patricia. "Where are you," he asked. He listened for a moment and then stared at his son. Unlike Max, Patricia talked a lot. Her father listened for several minutes and then hung up the phone. Max was the one.

For the first time in their married life Jack found Susan to be completely wrong about something. She should've paid closer attention to Max. On the upside Jack figured his wife loved surprises. This one would kill her. He couldn't take his eyes off Max.

"Max, did you know we weren't going to catch grayling?" Max offered his dad a sheepish grin and sent a little hello wave with his finger tips.

Chapter 7

Susan slept away the afternoon in the motel. Tired Patricia hadn't adjusted to her mother's odd sleep pattern and grabbed broken pieces of naps whenever she could throughout the days and nights. She had been dozing when her mother's restless thrashing woke her.

The constant barrage of turbulent emotions that endlessly bathed the woman rained down upon her compassionate soul. Over the years she learned to filter the malevolent impressions; otherwise the overload may have driven her mad. She knew she couldn't possibly solve all the ills of the world and so took an opportunistic approach, prioritizing her attention on those familiar or often nearby environments that were the loudest, causing the greatest harm to children.

Deep in Susan's sleep the creature within stirred. The witch smelled something bad, bad enough to get her attention. Knife awoke as Susan slept on.

The best maintained orphanages, though staffed by sympathetic caretakers, remain a heartbreaking solution, housing babies and children who have been deserted, left in the world on their own by circumstances not of their own making. Having been orphaned at sixteen, Susan was particularly sensitive to the loneliness and stigma uniquely suffered by orphans. Regardless of any good fortune that may come their way in the future, many would always carry the stain of the unwanted. The witch Knife wouldn't hesitate to unleash her fury on anyone who added to their burden.

Eleanor Didaldi, the director of The Riverview Children's Retreat, had unresolved childhood issues that should have precluded her from consideration as the head of an orphanage, a position she considered a job and nothing more. She had a temper and would randomly lash out to keep the children as well as the staff terrified, just as she intended. She felt it her mission to provide a structured, predictable environment, for herself.

In all fairness, the director had been badly beaten as a child by her mother. She too was a victim of the cycle of child abuse, an immutable, unfortunate imprinting that resulted in her being a beater as well. The sharp sting from a steel yardstick on the knuckles was the least of her corporal punishments to insure her trouble free day. The children in her charge didn't have to do anything wrong to earn her anger; asking for something was a sufficient transgression. As far as she was concerned they had food and a bed and that was enough. Anything else they would have to get for themselves when they reached their majority at eighteen and turned out into the world with a paper bag carrying one set of used clothing. Whatever else they may have acquired remained the property of the institution and had to be left behind to be reused by the remaining children. As far as she was concerned she had given them order and discipline and that was more than adequate for them to make their way without being a bother to humanity as some had been to her.

The orphan Jason Smith was a sensitive twelve-year-old free spirit, a good looking boy quite big for his age. Free spirits are born. They chart their own course without the compass of existing example. We know who they are when we see one. There is a fearless I-don't-care charisma about each that makes us admire their independent, creative invention. But in some instances it leads to envy disease, especially from those who conform without question in much the same way that many religious extremists are angered by non-believers. Such people demand submission to their dogma as though any other conviction would lessen the truth of their beliefs. The director was that rigid and she despised the free-spirited boy. For years she singled him out to get back at the memory of her mother, yet he remained unbroken and spirited.

Until the age of five Jason's name was Sunday March, the day of the week and the month that he had been abandoned to a hospital nursery, maybe a day old. Though his original birth certificate would always read Sunday March, the institution legally changed his name when he turned five as was their custom. A number of the other children in the orphanage had started out with calendar names. They all ended up as unrelated Smiths.

While Susan Stanich was sleeping, Jason found a dead bug in the lunch meal. Instead of quietly bringing it to the attention of the kitchen staff, he proudly displayed the bug to the other children at his table. His discovery echoed through the dining hall. Soon all of the children were searching their lunch, refusing to eat further. Several of the children let their imaginations run wild and threw up. That in turn triggered an empathetic reaction and more children began regurgitating their lunch. At that point the director walked into the lunchroom to find half the children vomiting and Jason Smith laughing his head off.

The woman took him into her office, closed the door and beat him, and beat him. The boy took it in silence, as stoic as he had been the many times she had whipped him before. But this time the woman completely lost her balance and her rage became unhinged. She was hurting him, really hurting him. It wasn't in his nature to do anything to stop her. In a bizarre twist of nature she was the only mother he had ever known and her authority was like God. But the energy from his pain was free to flow beyond the orphanage and out into the universe.

Time and distance folded together. Susan Stanich's eyes flew open even as she remained in a deep sleep. When she closed her eyes again she found herself in the director's office at the orphanage taking in the ugly scene. 'Bitch,' she thought. Violence was anathema to the witch but she decided to make an exception in this instance and slipped into the boy.

Jason Smith never remembered turning around and punching the director in her mouth. He couldn't because he wasn't the one who did it, not really. Shocked, the director dropped the hardwood switch she'd been using on Jason as she fell to the ground. He picked it up. Jason put a hard look on the director. They both knew what was coming, and he lay into her, rather the witch within did and Knife was really pissed off. The witch beat her just as the woman had beaten the boy, with every bit as much anger and force, and she had strength; the boy was big.

Susan Stanich bolted upright from her bed, scaring the hell out of Patricia who was now suddenly wide awake in spite of her exhaustion from lack of sleep.

"We're going to stay here another day," she said to Patricia.

"Electricity again....energy? Hmmm?"

"We're going to juvenile court. I have a surprise for you."

"I don't want to know."

Few people sat on the long wooden benches of the mostly empty gallery in Juvenile Court, likely the parents or other relatives lending support to the occupant of the defendant's table. The woman who presided over the courtroom had a no nonsense countenance balanced with kind, inquisitive eyes, perhaps a descriptive cliché but there she was, exuding a parental fairness well suited to her appointment to juvenile court. Her primary concern truly was the welfare of children while her responsibility to protect society from potentially dangerous individuals remained a somber consideration. She listened, she asked, she made decisions. Sleepless nights re-visiting difficult verdicts that could negatively impact a child's future attested to the seriousness with which she took her duty.

Over the course of the morning most of those charged were released to relatives; others were accompanied by a court officer through a door that meant incarceration as a youthful offender. Each case was preceded by the arrival of fresh worried faces and the departure of those whose child's fate had just been decided. Almost all of the relatives were teary eyed, some with relief, others because they were despondent. Like the accused children, they came and went.

The same overloaded public defender team acted on behalf of many of the defendants, closing one folder and opening another. In some cases the youths were accompanied by an advocate of the Child Protection Agency. The families of several had the means to hire their own lawyer. Jason Smith wasn't one of them. He had no idea why he was there. He remembered little from the events of the day before. One minute he was being beaten and the next the orphanage director was sitting on the floor bleeding, begging him to stop. He had no idea how the hardwood switch got in his hands. The director screamed when he tried to give it back to her. She was now sitting on the prosecution side of the gallery glaring at him through bandages when he entered the courtroom accompanied by a court officer who sat him at the defendant's table.

Susan Stanich, dragging Patricia behind her, walked into the courtroom and sat behind Jason Smith in time to hear the public defender's opening statement asking for leniency as it was the boy's first offense. Susan seethed with that presumption of guilt but she contained her rage. She had a flair for the dramatic at times and thought it best to hold her ace until it would have maximum impact.

The judge spent several minutes thumbing through a legal binder, stopping in several places to read entries that caught her attention, and then addressed the boy: "Jason, why in the world did you beat up Ms. Didaldi?" The boy shrugged his shoulders but said nothing.

"Jason," said the judge, "we're trying to be fair here. We're trying our best to understand why you did this. Can you please help me?"

Didaldi stood and burst out: "He attacked me. He's always been a troublesome child but I never thought he would do something like this. He belongs in prison."

"Your turn will come," said the judge and the director sat. "We don't put children in prison."

"There's no reason for this to continue," said Susan quietly, rushing the hearing so as not to be in the presence of the bitch longer than necessary. She'd had enough.

"And who are you?" asked the judge. "Unless I'm mistaken it's not your turn either. Just what stake do you have in these proceedings?"

"I'm the one who's going to adopt Jason Smith." Susan turned to the child, who was now looking at her with mouth agape. "Jason, I want you to take off your shirt." And then to the judge: "Please, humor me your honor. It'll be worth it."

"That woman has no business here." yelled Didaldi.

"I hate repeating myself," said the judge to Didaldi. Then the judge looked at Susan. There was steel on fire in Susan's blue-blue eyes. "Let's humor her."

"Jason, you must trust me," said Susan. "Take off your shirt. Then stand and look at me."

The boy hesitated for a long moment, and then the free spirit stood, faced Susan Stanich and removed his shirt. Susan looked at the judge whose stare was fixed on Jason's back. Some of the welts were fresh from the previous day's beating but the many bruises and slight scars proved a history of physical abuse.

Susan fixed on Didaldi. "Jason did more than beat you. He stopped you. Do you know the legal definition of self-defense?" And then to the judge: "Your honor, that individual has no business running an orphanage. She should be prosecuted for criminal endangerment of children. With the court's permission, I'm asking that the charges against Jason Smith be dismissed and for the court to place this child in my custody. I want him. We will be moving on to Washington State but will make ourselves available for any future proceedings. I can provide whatever security and references you require." Susan hoped the judge would see the wisdom in what she asked so she wouldn't have to pay her a visit later that night. And that was that.

As they left the courthouse Susan asked Jason how he felt about changing his name back to Sunday March: "A unique name for an unusual boy, fitting," she said with a warm Susan smile.

"How did you know my name was Sunday March?"

"I know everything."

"She does," said Patricia, "a real pain in the ass but you'll get used to it."

"Sunday March," said Susan, "you are no longer an orphan. You're mine."

It had been more than a week since Alice Summers had been kidnapped and she was beginning to feel right at home. She figured the longer she stayed kidnapped the more dramatic her return, the bigger the spotlight. You couldn't pry her out of that basement without a Hollywood contract in hand.

In a reversal of fortunes it was the kidnapper who was under her spell, falling madly in love with Alice. When he interspersed 'honey' and 'sweetheart' with 'Alice' he meant it. Good food, good company; what more could Alice ask for, except maybe that contract. She'll probably get it someday. If someone else scores first, Alice will undoubtedly take it from her.

In an unfortunate plight for the males of the world, Alice Summers is that attractive, a striking, classic face and a woman's body, in addition to being a little wacky and obsessed with ambition...all this in the hands of a manipulative seventeen-year-old. It's easy to see why she couldn't help torturing the opposite sex. Conveniently, most males enjoy being humiliated when competing for the attention of a beautiful, overtly fucked up lovebird, even when she comes wrapped in emasculation. Stunning beauty does that, distorts the perspective of some the same way too much money skews reality for others. The kidnapper was miserable, and devoted.

His routine in prior abductions had been to seduce his victims with dash and kindness, waiting on their every desire to remove any hint of threat and put them at ease, completely trusting him. He never made a move on a one of them without a clear invitation. Besides DVDs of x-rated romantic comedies to speed thing along, he filled their days with readings of amorous poetry and prose, and flooded the basement with boudoir jazz day and night. The only thing missing may have been directions to the bedroom and an instructional manual with workbook when they got there, if they needed one. After a time the victims felt as though they were being rushed for the world's most popular sorority, his baby-factory, and they liked it. His full court press took weeks, sometimes a month, but had always worked. In Alice's case he ramped up his efforts to crushing grovel, which in the ensuing days would yield absolutely nothing, not even an innocent handshake, which he tried. Nothing turned Alice off more than a needy suitor. She was disgusted with him.

Television quickly became a bore. Board games got thin. But teasing the kidnapper was entertainment without end. Tormenting fellow cast members who fell under Alice's charm had been her favorite until she met the kidnapper. He was more fun than an acting class full of horny teen-agers. There was absolutely no way she was leaving, or loving.

It usually took several months before the kidnapper felt confident that he could leave the doors unlocked and give his victims free rein to come and go as they pleased. In Alice's case he was ready to give her keys to his car in less than a week because she gave him little more than pity and aggravation. She could even keep the car. He was so ashamed of his lack of control over the situation that he considered moving and just leaving her there, but he couldn't bear to be without her, not yet. He even enjoyed the viscious belittling and henpecking. It was attention.

By the beginning of the second week the kidnapper had exhausted his coping mechanisms. Though not overly brilliant in spite of the Mensa claim, he was smart enough to know that Alice was more than he could handle; self-preservation and all that. The monthly call wasn't scheduled yet but he broke protocol and called his mother two weeks early. Alice joined him, masked as always, on the nighttime ride to a location where they couldn't be traced. By the end of the week he would insist Alice begin calling her mother as well. And he would join her. He'd listen to anyone who could help him stay out of jail and get rid of her. The kidnapping degenerated into a web of competing family interests from which they would spend the following months trying to extricate themselves. The dilemma was a comic book.

The kidnapper could be the poster child for a mama's boy, which helps explain his distorted opinion of his gene pool. Home schooled so as not to be tainted by outside influences, he was spoiled, which is not the same as being pampered. All children should be pampered. Why not? But spoiled is synonymous with rotten. He wasn't merely the center of the world; he was the world, which made two of them, counting Alice.

His zany mother made sure he thought he was a prince. She worshipped him; shouldn't everyone? The woman was delighted that he was spreading his royal seed, propagating the family's special genes. As a matter of fact it was her idea. She wanted lots of grandchildren. Child abuse comes is different flavors. In this case it was deranged devil's food. Though Susan Stanich would never be able to sense Alice or the kidnapper on ethereal winds, she could feel the zing of the mother's zig-zag vibrations, an irritation she couldn't quite pinpoint like a maddening mosquito in a dark bedroom.

The last several days of the ride west were deliberately uneventful. Susan knew what Sunday March required and made sure absolutely nothing happened outside of sightseeing, good food and a warm bed in his own motel room. They didn't talk about the future or the past. They just let the present soak in. Patricia spent the days staring in wonderment at the back of her mother's head and took an immediate liking to Sunday. Anyone would. Sunday March's mouth caught flies and his eyes were blinkless. He was stuck in disbelief, his mind incapable of grasping his good fortune. Bounced around in foster homes since birth, he gave up on real adoption when barely five. Adoptive parents always wanted the babies and all the children knew it. The older the orphan the less likely adoption, which for the older children became Oz, make believe. They viewed foster homes as a poor child's adoption, often resulting in a return to the orphanage. Adoption was different and no one came back. Susan felt the world owed Sunday a great deal and she was intent on making sure he would get it all.

To celebrate their crossing of the continental divide as they approached Idaho, Patricia pelted Susan with endless questions now that the door had been opened to a hint of her mother's secrets. Susan, as usual, parried all questions with replies whose purpose was to prepare Patricia for her independence, which is the responsibility of all mothers, and fathers. Sunday March listened but the life lessons Susan offered went in one ear and out the other, He was still a boy and went back to spending his time day dreaming about a recently discovered interest changing shape right in front of his pre-adolescent eyes; girls.

"How did you end up in Santa Cruz?" daughter asked mother.

"Surfing. I like to surf, right? Where better?"

"But you can't surf much in Washington."

"Nope, that's life. We had to leave Santa Cruz and the great surfing because you let yourself get kidnapped."

"It wasn't my fault."

"Yes, it was. I told you to come straight home. You didn't listen."

"She was my teacher."

"So, I guess that was a lesson you hadn't planned on learning, right? Life's a swirl of serious and silly. Children are serious. Anything that helps make them healthy and keeps them safe is serious. Everything else is light stuff, filler. Surfing is fun but it's not serious. Outside of preparing children to survive so that they can do the same thing to the next generation, all else should be a kind of waiting game filled with diversions and entertainment, pleasures, silliness. Why not? It's about evolution Patricia. All life is moving in a direction. We've no idea the end game but the direction is clear and evolution is taking us there. Humanity's brain power is increasing, not enough to see the change even when we stand still, but if we go back to see where we've come from the evidence is undeniable. It's about evolution and children are needed for that. You, Max and now Sunday March are serious business."

"What," said Sunday March upon hearing his name.

"Mind your own business," said Susan.

"How do you know all this?" asked Patricia.

"My mother told me."

"Did you ask her how she knew?"

"I couldn't. She was dead when she told me. Look, there's some other things I want you to know. Sunday March, you can listen in on this too."

"Sunny, call me Sunny. Sunday March sounds stupid.

"Nope, to me you're Sunday March. Everyone else can call you Sunny, but not me."

"Then call Patricia, Patricia March."

"Sunday March, shut up and listen. No talking, no discussion. Say okay." Together they said okay. It wasn't wise to irritate Susan.

"Death addicts are all around us. The laws are wrong. Laws look for motive. That's not why people kill. The predisposition to kill lurks in their personality, maybe from something in their brain when they're born, more likely the result of abuse, even more likely a result of abuse triggering an anger gene. But that gene could just as easily have been channeled to a productive life where ambition leads to something productive. Do you understand what I am saying? Yes or no?"They both said yes.

"Smart kids. It's inherited."

"We're not related," said Sunday March.

"Yeah, but you're so smart you should've been. So, back to death addicts. Eloise DeMarco, the one Patricia nailed to a floor, was a death addict."

"You nailed someone to a floor?" said Sunday.

"It was so long ago I almost forgot I did it, until mom reminded me, just now," replied Patricia. "Don't get me angry and you have nothing to worry about."

"Oh, man, you people are starting to scare me," said Sunday, but he didn't really mean it. Actually he found the new information reassuring. "This is like being a member of the toughest gang in the neighborhood."

"Back to shut up," said Susan. And he did. "Wars are the work of death addicts. Territory, religion, greed...none of it has anything to do with why countries wage war. War is always started by a death addict leading a gang of death addicted bullies. Regardless of the motive that instigates a war, it's always a ruse, an excuse. It's always bullies intent on killing because killing is the only thing that makes them feel better. It's very simple and very sad. Until the world deals with war on that level there will be wars. We have a long way to go. Don't ever trust any politician. Don't believe a word they say. It's possible there could be a good one in the bunch but it's better to distrust all of them. 99% of them are obsessed with wielding power, nothing more. When power addicts migrate to death addiction we have war. All the wars in the history of mankind have been instigated and orchestrated by a few hundred death addicted assholes. That's why democracy may be best of the worst. We can always vote the death addicts out before it's too late. Democracy keeps the power base in the hands of the people, keeps shuffling the deck with elections so no one individual or group can get too much power. More often than not the majority of people will smell rats before too much damage is done and elect them out. Even then it's pretty tricky. Shit happens and people get fooled. Again, it's best not to trust anyone seeking power, not a one of them. Amen."

Chapter 8

Back home in Washington, try as she might and focusing all of her attention, Susan Stanich remained unable to sense Alice Summers and refused to talk with Detectives Pasquale or Millman; there was nothing to tell them. She studied photos of the girl and spent hours talking with Alice's parents who, by the fourth week and unbeknownst to Susan or the police, had been negotiating with their daughter her conditions for returning home. Car, cell phone, trip to Europe....each time her parents said yes to her demands, she added another. She wasn't going home. No way. The girl was a merciless, calculating force of nature.

Susan couldn't figure why she didn't feel what should have been a torrent of emotion from the kidnapping. She also couldn't figure out what was up with Jack. There was an elephant in the room and a grin stuck on his face hiding something. She figured it must have something to do with trout and pursued whatever it was not at all, which is the way Jack figured things would play out and his grin got wider. The twinkle in Max's eyes got more sparkly, which passed her by completely. The impressions that usually came to her were dark in nature; the darker the sensation the deeper the mark. She didn't read minds. That would drive anyone crazy, burdened with the constant barrage of the garbage that goes through the minds of a million souls, ten million. The forces about, whatever they are, created her brain in such a way as to filter intake, just as we can only do one thing at a time in spite of the trendy multi-tasking fairy tale. She wasn't a know-it-all. She only felt some things and had no idea why or how.

The Sunday March adjustment was a situation comedy with a child impossible not to love. For any other boy the Stanich home may have been another country, requiring time to learn the language and customs. Not so with shy-less Sunday. He'd imagined what a real home would be like in his mind so many times that he set about recreating his dream as soon as he walked across the threshold, immediately making himself comfortable rearranging the furniture in the room Susan had made his. He then provided her with a prioritized list of what else he wanted. Though the free-spirited child was adorable and warm, the sort of boy that could make anyone lighter just by looking in his direction, there was one slight quirk that the Stanichs hadn't foreseen. As such it was the Stanichs who would have to make the adjustment.

It seems he brought into their home the unwritten rules of The Riverview Children's Retreat, the first of which is also embedded into the common law legal code: possession is nine tenths of the law. Sunday March was and is a thief without conscience, a very good one. So he happily stole whatever he saw and then it was his. Selfish didn't have meaning to the former orphan, or corporate CEOs for that matter. They are their only world and as such whatever they acquire is theirs unless someone steals it back. The concept of sharing never entered Sunday's mind, barter yes, share no. So, he took everything in sight and moved the bounty into the room that was now his: tennis rackets, jackets, fishing rods, two MP3 players, etc. Half the house found its way onto his floor, table tops, and in his drawers and closet. Susan, Jack, Patricia and Max watched in wonder as their possessions disappeared fully aware he was the culprit. But he was an excellent thief, a natural. At no time did they catch him and they tried, even took turns guarding him. Sunday still pulled it off right in front of their eyes. Susan was convinced he could slip a television up his sleeve and they'd never see a thing.

He transferred the kitchen pantry to his dresser and anywhere else he could find space. Within days his room looked like a mini-market. So, the Stanichs got together and did a Solomon thing and decided to let him keep everything he took if that's what he required and then retrieve their possessions when needed, an endless parade deliberately intruding on his space. Thereafter, if Max wanted his baseball bat back he would politely knock on Sunday's door, ask for the bat and then return it when he was done. Grocery shopping became more convenient because Sunday's room was closer to the front door than the kitchen. Food stocks, with the exception of refrigerated items, were unloaded on his bed. Mealtimes were especially irritating to Sunday. The Stanich clan made it a point to individually retrieve the salt shaker he'd hoarded, one at a time, and then set it back. Eventually the ill-wisdom of his compulsion to steal came to him. By the week's end Sunday almost but not quite figured out the new world and put everything back in place so people would stop knocking on his door and going in and out of his room, about which he became quite possessive. Then Susan spoke with him.

"Sunday, everything here is yours. You don't have to steal or hoard anything. The only thing we value is ourselves and that includes you. You want something just ask."

"You gotta be kidding. Can I have the car?"

"No. And if you touch it I'll break your fucking head. Deal?"

"You would, wouldn't you?" Susan gave him a sweet smile so he'd know she would.

And so Sunday March learned that it wasn't necessary to steal, from the Stanichs anyway.

A few days after Susan's return Jack felt it best to figuratively spill the beans during lunch, a bit concerned about what Max might get into if left on his own any longer. Patricia had taken Sunday March to a movie, an invitation that Max deferred so he could be at his official unveiling. He loved surprises. His mother didn't but she could smell a conspiracy the same as anyone else.

"Please pass the salt," said Jack.

"What is it?" said Susan as she handed over the shaker she had pinched back from Sunday's room for the meal. "Are you and Max having some monster trout mounted? What's going on here? Let's have it."

"All we caught was bait," said Max.

"Which one of you wants to die first?" she said. "What's going on? Don't make me say fuck."

"It's Max," said Jack.

"What's Max?"

"It's Max, not Patricia, what you were worried about." Susan had no idea what he was referring to. She looked at Jack and he nodded towards Max. She looked at Max and then back to Jack. "Susan, it's Max. He's the one."

"Jesus Christ, not Max."

Susan Stanich was wrong. It was inherited or maybe Max shared her predisposition for the gift but her child's life would not be the normal one she had hoped. There's always a price to be paid for the awakened. The ability was a double-edged sword. Susan knew some of what lay ahead for Max and the tears fell. When Jack saw her reaction his heart opened and his tears joined hers.

She had a lot on her mind and concluded maybe she had been on overload: There was Sunday March, folding him into the family; and the ebbing trauma from her return to New York; and concern regarding Patricia's ability to absorb her mother's history; and the daily deflections of phone calls from the Seattle police. How else could she possibly have missed something as big as Max? But, again, she was looking in the wrong place. Like we said, the energy from laughter goes right over her head. As such she had been surrounded by bubble machines, until now.

Susan wiped the tears from her face. "Jack something else has come up. I have to go out for a while." She got up and walked into Sunday's room and placed the salt shaker back under his bed.

While all this was going on Janice Goldman was slowly reeling in a Lou Pasquale fish. She could have taught Jack Stanich a thing or two about grayling as well. Fortunately, the burgeoning relationship with his future bride was a sufficient distraction to allow Lou mental breaks in trying to catch Susan Stanich flying through the air. Susan wished she could fly just to make him happy but she can't fly, no one can. It's all in the mind though actually flying through the air would be far easier to comprehend or explain.

It was a full month after the Summers girl vanished when Ms. Goldman saw that look in Lou's eyes again. It was 10:30 pm. They'd just finished the after dinner tawny port and were about to practice pre-marital sex when Lou's cell phone did its thing. Lou became Detective Pasquale and it was goodbye Janice.

The bizarre kidnapping of Alice Summers took a back seat when a fifteen-year-old child staggered into the emergency room of a hospital severely beaten, near dead from the loss of blood. Pasquale met Millman at the hospital just when the vascular surgeon walked out of the operating room. He'd also just arrived, peeked in on the situation and was on his way to prep for surgery. It was going to be a long night.

"It's an accident that she's alive," said the surgeon. "Whoever beat her meant to cut the jugular veins. The moron didn't know where they were and missed. Lucky girl. But he hit her vocal chords. She won't be talking for a while. After surgery we'll be keeping her in an induced coma for the time being."

Unfortunately that same night two other girls had been beaten and slashed, a fourteen and a sixteen-year-old. They weren't so lucky. They died. This, Susan felt. And all the bubbles burst.

Lou Pasquale strode into the precinct to find Susan Stanich pacing the floor waiting for him. Millman sat at his desk watching. He'd tried getting conversation from the woman. Nothing. Buried in deep thought she didn't look up until she heard Pasquale's footsteps approach.

"I know," she said as he drew near. He wore a very worried look.

"What do you know? And how long have you been back? We've been trying to reach you for two weeks."

"I didn't have anything to say."

"Now you got something to say?" asked Pasquale.

"The rest were just choir boys. This is why you were meant to find me. That's what I know."

"What else do you know?"

"Nothing. There's nothing except pain."

"That's it, just pain?"

"Yeah, and the painkiller, death. That's what I know, pain and death. Human sacrifice."

"What are you talking about?"

"It's always human sacrifice. Murder, wars, revenge killings, honor killings...you name it. Death addicts are always committing human sacrifice regardless of the setting or excuse. The demise of another is a catalyst that will somehow alleviate pain, deprivation or bring a better life in the here and now. Want more crops, kill someone. Need rain, do a virgin. Sometimes whole countries feel cranky so they drop some bombs and feel new and improved. It's all about human sacrifice no matter how you slice it; killing to make it better. Think about it."

"I'm glad you're here," he said.

"I'm not," she replied.

"How about we grab a cup of coffee?"

"I don't drink coffee."

"Tea?"

"Green tea?"

"We got. C'mon." Millman followed along.

Chapter 9

The only person he could ever count on was in the mirror and then only sometimes. He knew there was something wrong with him and accepted that his mind wasn't right. Crazy people know they're crazy. They usually keep it to themselves though some brag to intimidate or manipulate, but they're never believed until it's too late.

George Adamson was pretty, blessed with a naturally slender physique and a beguiling baby face flashing beautiful green eyes. Medium length blond hair was cut to bangs, clearly meant to be androgynous. Though well into his thirties he could easily pass for someone in their late teens; his effeminate face unnaturally hairless as a result of extensive laser treatments. Each morning he attended his appearance as though he were the featured model in an upscale photo shoot for a GQ spread on the perfect youthful face. Dozens of expensive domestic and imported skin cleansers sat on shelves. Always dissatisfied with the previous day's result, each morning he would scan his collection and invariably settle on the product that hadn't been used the longest. Custom blended moisturizers prepared by a cosmetologist exclusively for his skin tone lent a radiant glow to his face. He had been assured the elixir was available nowhere else. The resulting effect was too immaculate, complemented by attire comparably too right. His smooth, innocent countenance, though exaggerated, appeared disarmingly harmless. He was not.

He was a killer. When he did the deed there was a brief reprieve from the endless pain and sadness he suffered. Killing felt good.

Though they were alive and well, he knew neither mother nor father yet wasn't an orphan or adopted, rather something else spawned by absentee parenting that hasn't yet been defined. The trust-fund baby George Adamson was born into a wealthy family as a result of an inbreeding marriage of sorts between first cousins, neither of whom wanted children because they shared with no one, not even themselves. They each inherited what was theirs prior to the marriage and intended to hold on tight for the duration. When the inbred accident made his appearance they pretended he never happened. It wasn't that they didn't like him. They just didn't want to be bothered, overwhelmingly selfish as only the damaged_uber rich are capable. The rest of us need one another. As long as his birth made no further demands on them his existence was of no concern. He knew they were his parents because that's what he was told, but as a child he had no idea what that meant. He saw his mother and father briefly on only several occasions. When he was ten, he passed their car as he was being driven from the family compound. He thought his mother looked at him but it could have been wishful thinking.

Childhood was a succession of nannies, boarding schools and Summer camps. His home address for legal and mailing purposes was the spacial mansion on the compound in Puget Sound. He'd been allowed to visit there only a few times before he reached his twenty-first birthday, at which age he was provided with a luxury condo and enough coupon money to spend the rest of his life doing nothing if that's what he wanted, on the one condition that he never visit the island. All he would ever know of the compound was that his parents, whoever they were, sometimes lived there. From the day he was born until the present he'd never had a loving hand touch him nor heard a comforting word. For the thirty-three years of his life he had been left alone in a sterile world that didn't want or need him, stuck in unwanted childhood.

Over time the isolation and rejection relentlessly fed upon itself and morphed into unbearable emotional pain without relief, and madness. Reality checks were non-existent so George Adamson created myths, painkillers of sorts to make reason of his lot in life. In particular, he was convinced that his parents would have wanted him had he been female, which is why his hatred was directed towards girls, a bent case of lethal sibling rivalry.

Like many psychopaths, Adamson's intellect was a brilliant, narrowly focused funnel; mental energy escapes through available outlets. His was solely occupied with fending off his compulsion to kill until the obsession overwhelmed him. Regardless, only death occupied his mind. His trail of killing had been carefully spaced in time and method in a deliberate attempt to thwart any pattern that could be discernible and potentially lead to his discovery and capture. Self control was a game he played with himself, limited to seeing how long he could go before the compulsion took over, and that pause was becoming shorter and shorter. This time, the previous night, completely enveloped in hurt, he went on a spree. It took three beatings and slashings before his anxiety released in a rush, subsiding to relative painlessness for the time being. But killing was a drug for George Adamson and he was addicted. Dead people were his fix.

Susan Stanich could smell him. His black energy during the night of the killings had taken over her senses. In the aftermath ghosted vibrations remained swirling in her mind like dirt you can neither see nor wash off.

“**W**ho are you?” Pasquale asked Susan two days later. They were seated in the small lunchroom at the police station. “Is Packard your real name or that another pseudonym? Why did you change your name? Why do I have all these deviants reporting crazy things about you?”

“Please don’t tell me you think I fly through the air,” replied Susan. She looked over at Millman. He just rolled his eyes.

“I don’t know what I think. How did you find all those perverts?”

“This is so simple. There’s web sites full of whoever you’re looking for. Start with one or two in a chatroom and they’ll lead you to the rest. Then I hacked into their computers. You can’t but I can. What are they going to do, sue me for catching them with their pants down? They all knew each other and I got to know all of them. I scare the shit out of them. No magic. Is that so hard to understand? How come your partner never talks?”

“Sometimes I can’t get him to shut up. This isn’t one of them. Why do I have two who swear they saw you fly?”

“And you believe them? You actually think I can fly through the air. Lou, you’re losing it. It’s all in their minds, nothing more.”

“You get into their minds, don’t you?”

“Of course. Don’t we get into each other’s minds all the time. I’ve been in your mind. I know it. You put me there.

There's nothing more to it than that. Now, who are we looking for?"

"Don't you know?"

"Lou...I ain't calling you Detective anything. It takes too long to say. So, Lou, if I knew that I would tell us, now wouldn't I?"

"Gimme some maybes."

"He's different. He...the surviving girl did say it was a he, yes?

"She's still out of it. Can't talk anyway, not for awhile," said Millman.

"See, my partner talks," said Pasquale.

"I'm certain it's a he," said Susan. "Don't ask how I know. He's angry and he's alone. So, right away we can eliminate women and married men. Figure a 100 miles radius. Those are our suspects."

"That's the best you can do?"

"Maybe. Look, I need some time to clear my plate. I'll get back to you."

"I still want to know who you are." Susan was silent, hard eyes fixed on Pasquale, then Millman, and Knife came out.

"I am Sandra DeSantos, from the South Bronx, your neighborhood. When I was 16 a scumbag raped and cut me. He cut me bad, really pissed me off. He got dead but I'm still pissed off. Someone hurts a kid I go bananas. You've no fucking idea. Look Dudley, everything I do is legit unless you can prove otherwise. That's all I'll ever tell you and that's all you need to know. And if I am who you imagine I am don't you think it would be a good idea to fuck off. "

"No more of that Dudley crap," Pasquale said as he watched Susan Stanich walk past him and leave. Then he jumped on his computer and began a search through police records to see if there had ever been a Sandra DeSantos in The Bronx. Fortunately for Pasquale there were no computerized birth and school records that old listing a Sandra DeSantos around the age of Susan. If there were and he had followed up she would've been really really pissed off. He let it lie. Millman just watched the proceedings. Speculation and broomsticks weren't his thing. His comfort level insisted of facts he could see or touch.

"**W**hose turn is it to watch Max?" asked Susan. Jack was cooking, another 'Guess what you'll eat tonight' night.

Max was such a quiet child it was hard for anyone to tell what was going on in his mind. Even Susan, who shared pieces of his gift, had no idea. She and Jack decided that for the time being it would be best if they kept a tighter rein on Max. Susan felt he was way too young to deal with the input that must be coming his way without a little guidance, a mother hen's concern, same as nudging Patricia towards her maturity, only with something added. Susan had no way of knowing how the forces about favored Max, or with what insights or powers, or what fell upon his spirit. How was he weighted down by knowing more than his peers? Could he handle it? What of his loneliness? The knowing wasn't a thing that is disclosed, not to anyone. She knew all too well that what comes through such consciousness doesn't get voiced.

"Your turn," said Jack. "I've been on the past two weeks. That was the deal."

"Good start, time for a new deal."

Jack thought for a moment and said, "Okay, sure." That was the extent of their argument. Maybe it happened so fast you missed it. They got along that well, never worked at it.

Susan shielded Jack from what she would always refer to as a project. She said no more and he asked nothing. That was the understanding. That she was a magnet for negative energy she kept to herself. It was her burden alone. Jack wasn't oblivious to his extraordinary wife's ways. He knew something but never what. From the time they met he instinctively kept the distance she required when she needed it. In bed, of course, things were quite different. She'd pretend he was in charge for the strutting fuel that he like most men require. Though Jack was perpetually in a state of teenage testosterone overload, when her hormones made their presence known she would throw him a hip when he'd least expect and off they'd go with Jack thinking it was his idea.

"Two girls are dead, a third in a hospital," she said. "I don't know what I can offer but that detective, the one who thinks I fly through the air wants me to help. I need some time. Whattaya say?"

"Go for it. Be careful. How long will it take? Take your broomstick."

"I don't know. Don't let Patricia torture the boys." Sunday March and Max had become an instant team. They both enjoyed initiating obligatory spats with Patricia. Susan and Jack figured the boys were outnumbered but stayed out of it. And that was that.

Chapter 10

The following morning Susan was back in the police station. Alice Summers's kidnapping was relegated to the back burner with assurances from Mrs. Stanich to Pasquale that the girl's well being was not a concern. Regular meetings with her parents would be procedure so they could be briefed as new information came their way, even if there was none. It struck Susan as odd that the parents' initial overwrought, rational concern dwindled to polite attendance during meetings at which Alice's mother and father seemed blasé at best. She eyed them suspiciously but got no hint of the negotiations taking place on the sidelines. Just the same, in her bones she felt the girl was fine. The kidnapper on the other hand was being driven to the verge of a nervous breakdown by Alice. But Susan didn't know that.

There was really no reason for Susan to physically come to the police station other than to soothe Pasquale and Millman with her presence. The unknown creates its own mysteries and as such it seemed to Susan they were attributing to her powers and abilities approaching the stuff of childish fairy tales, which under different circumstances would have provided entertainment. As she saw it she was just a simple run-of-the-mill witch and figured there had to be others like her though she had never run into any and concluded they must be as secretive as her. Just the same she was no superwoman, couldn't even fly through the air.

It was all in their minds like she kept saying. But some people just don't listen.

So, when they called again Mrs. Stanich good naturedly came over to comfort them knowing full well it would be unlikely that what she was looking for would be helped by anything they had to offer. When she drove up she could see them watching from the windows to see if she brought the killer with her. Once inside, they kept looking at her as though the killer's identification would suddenly pop into her head. They were a pain in the ass but she humored them because they could be a source of information. You never know.

As intended, and the result of the journey back to her origins, Susan Stanich's senses were now honed to a fine edge and expanding outwards as though the tentacles from sight, hearing and touch were reaching beyond her horizons and probing in all directions, bleeding into the world in search of a death addict, a being with a unique mental footprint, well aware that he possessed an uncontrollable compulsion to kill, someone who gave off nothing because all stimuli that came his way became internalized, a black hole of emotional communication; nothing normal escaped. The day-to-day swells of happiness or disappointment were absent from the energy that was emitted from his being.

Outside of war, violent death is rarely a planned thing, rather a spontaneous act instigated by a spike of momentary anger usually preceded by jealousy or insult. Not so with death addicts. Theirs may be a cold act without any external incident to trigger their response. For them the journey towards death is a calculated movement towards calm, soothing respite from the internal madness within which each is held captive in solitary confinement. There is no guilt or regret, rather gratitude for the release from pain. They've no more compassion for their victim than a headache would feel for an aspirin tablet. That detachment gives off its own distinct energy. And that's what Susan was looking for and there was nothing in the police station that would help in that search. She was seeking a dead zone that would be impossible to sense until it awoke and began emitting the sparks of insanity that would signal its stirring, hopefully providing a telltale trail she could follow to its source.

"Anything new?" asked Millman.

"Babies. Babies are new. Ever wonder why people say 'new baby'? Stanley, you know of any old babies?"

"You never let up, do you," said Pasquale.

"Oh, you mean do I have the killer outside in the car, maybe in the truck? Did I bring you his address? Is that what you're asking? Hmm? Aren't you the police? Shouldn't you be the ones with something new?"

"We heard you're adopting a boy," said Pasquale.

"He's not new, been around for years. Who told you?"

"He did when I called."

"Kid's got a big mouth. He'll fit right in. Fellas, it's been nice chatting with but I gotta be on my way now unless there's something else."

"That's it?" said Millman.

"Yep, got a busy day ahead of me."

"Doing what?" said Pasquale.

"My husband recently informed me that we'll need another broomstick." And Mrs. Stanich was out of there.

George Adamson awoke in a state of calm, not to be confused with peace. The killings merely blanketed his usual internal state of rage, the compulsion incubating in a more pleasant numb-land. No sparks escaped to scratch at Susan Stanich. But the news reports that one of his victims was alive became a ticking bomb.

Stepping from bed and into his slippers, he walked from his bedroom looking at himself in the large, full-length mirrors set upon the walls of his spacious home. There were no Picasso sketches, 18th century oils or contemporary trip-tychs of watercolors one might find decorating the halls of a posh condo. There were only mirrors, dozens of them. Wherever George looked he saw himself, his reflection confirmation that he existed because in the recesses of his damaged mind there was no one else he would trust who could provide that reassurance.

Adamson didn't shower, hadn't for several days, not wishing to wash away any of the events of the night that had brought with it a lessening of the perpetual anguish that filled his soul. And this day he would forego the usual ostentatious attire with which he typically set himself apart from others. This day he wanted to blend in. George was going to another funeral dressed in appropriate mourning attire. The day before he'd attended the funeral of one of his victims. He wanted to take in the sadness of the family and friends of his victims, to feed on the grief of others, their misery dessert after a satisfying meal and in so doing perpetuate for a time longer the external turmoil he had created to offset his own madness, a balancing act of sorts.

Hundreds attended the funeral, making him indistinguishable standing against a wall at the back of the church along with dozens of other unrelated attendees who may have been there out of compassion, or perhaps a universal thankfulness that the services could just as easily have been for one of them. Some came seeking a spectacle and, of course, there was local and network news coverage by journalists and photographers. Though Adamson was only a tree in the forest the images captured at the two funerals would become his fingerprints, not that it would help the police in the long run.

He stood there taking in the crying, the tears, the sobbing of mourners, each stab of someone else's pain a comfort to him. Only when the cortege left the funeral home did Adamson feel a genuine weight of sadness. For him it was it was over, too soon. He was left with himself again.

Once home, George could sense a creep far down a tunnel deep in his mind, not yet at the surface but waiting. It was coming on too quickly this time, faster than ever before and he wasn't ready, didn't want it but he could feel it there beginning to coil. The surviving girl was a path to his capture and the end of the only source of relief for the death addict Adamson. There hadn't been sufficient calm in the eye of the storm. He was like someone who didn't have quite enough soothing sleep but was now kept awake by an irritation he couldn't quite pinpoint. So, he reached for the distraction that had managed to take the edge off his rage many times before, since his late teens. George was a porn addict. Cruising internet chatrooms that serviced other deviants of a similar, sadistic bent was the setting and also the feeding grounds where he found and stalked his victims, and that's where he would stumble upon Susan Stanich or vice versa, or so it appeared for as we know there are no accidents. The universe does provide. In this case serendipity would arrive swinging a sword instead of singing a song.

Meanwhile back at the Alice Summers show, the star awoke the following morning deciding she no longer needed clothes. Her next act would be theatre in the nude, a command performance for the kidnapper. From that morning on the only thing she would wear would be a mask, sarcastic encore after encore, day after day.

When the kidnapper walked into the basement he stopped breathing.

"I want you to see what you're not getting," said Alice. "You touch me, I'll cut off your balls. When I decide to leave here I'm giving it to the first hot guy I meet, anyone but you."

"Because of me you're famous..."

"Oh, sure, like you planned it. I figured it out, not you stupid. The only time I'll put on clothes is when we drive to call my parents or that crazy mother of yours. But I won't be wearing underwear, no bra. Just so you should know. And my yoga you've been drooling over, same thing, naked."

"Okay, then I'll be naked too." And the kidnapper began to undress.

"If I see that weenie I'll cut it off," Alice said. And he pulled his pants back up. "Moron, boys have been exposing themselves to me since I was12. Boring, boring, boring. It's time for my aerobics. Put on the music. You can watch." Then the kidnapper's cell phone rang.

"No, one has this number except my mother. She would never call."

"It's for me," said Alice. "My mother. She's gonna tell me I can go to a private school for the performing arts in LA. Just let it ring. She'll call back. I guarantee it."

"Are you crazy? They'll find me."

"No they won't. She bought one of those temporary phones with fixed minutes. Untraceable. I told her if she didn't let me go away to school I would run away when they caught us and she'd never see me again. She's calling to beg me to go away to school like I want."

"You are crazy."

"Oh, please...I hate public school. I want to hang with talent. Besides I used up all the boys in my school. They are really so dumb, but a lot smarter than you." The two of them sat there staring at the cell phone Alice insisted he not answer as it rang in his hand. It briefly stopped, then began ringing again. "See, told you. Now you can answer it. Mom wants you to convince me to come home. She likes you...and hey, kidnapper, she makes beautiful, smart talented kids. The proof is right here in front of your eyes. Kidnap her next time. I'll set it up. Talk to her. When she stops crying give me the phone."

The kidnapper held the cell to his ear and listened. Several times he tried to get a word in but soon realized that would be fruitless. He did manage several 'uh huhs' when Alice's mother was forced to breathe. With that as encouragement the monologue continued until it appeared that there were no more tears, at which point he passed the phone to Alice.

"What ma?" said Alice. And then it was Alice's turn to listen, which eventually seemed to culminate in a deal of sorts: "So, let me get this straight, you're willing to let me go to school in LA. I'll have my own car, a new one and red, right? RIGHT?...Ok, this is a start. I'll think it over. I need the cell number of that woman you've been talking to so I can arrange coverage of my return from the terrible ordeal of this kidnapping. No rush. Call me back when you have the number." Alice ended the call and handed the cell back to the kidnapper, "Now we're getting somewhere."

While that was going on the Stanich boys were enjoying the afternoon lounging around a coffee shop in downtown Bellingham, checking out retro hippie teeny boppers who were working hard to get stared at so they could act offended. The boys had biked to a bus stop from the house and from there to within a block of the sidewalk cafe. After about an hour, boredom took sway and Max got an idea, threw an affectionate arm around Sunday March, "Sunday, whattaya say we get rich? You up for that?"

"Your mother said I shouldn't listen when you get an idea."

"Don't worry. We'll give her some. Everyone'll get a share. You get extra because I'm letting you in on the ground floor. You in?" The Stanich gleam is contagious. Besides, Sunday March had a decent gleam of his own to add to their glow. He didn't know what was up but he was sure it would be a gem.

"I'm in," said Sunday, "but this better not screw up my adoption."

"Mom said you're my brother," said Max. "So you're my brother. Don't worry. You're gonna love this. Tomorrow we're taking a bus down to Burlington."

"What's in Burlington?" asked Sunday, almost afraid to hear the answer.

"Off track betting," said Max. "How much money have you saved?"

"Your mother was right," said Sunday.

"Don't worry. She's gonna love this."

Initially, chatroom perverts know each other only by unimaginative pseudonyms. As such, participants in any of the many the punk, tattoo and S&M web sites Adamson frequented went by handles like Satanette, Devilman, Whipper, Leatherbeast, etc. The names weren't very inventive, creativity being limited to group fantasies about virtually any deviation sufficiently from the norm to engage their imaginations as they skirted their fantasies, the closer to forbidden taboos the better. Asking for real names or e-mail addresses was taboo. If a newcomer were to accidentally broach that prohibition he would become persona non grata and ignored.

Adamson changed his name more often than a check forger. Killer13 was the current alias, his idea of dancing on the edge with in-your-face candor that would never be conceived as possible by others on the site. Susan Stanich went by Witch Woman. When you think about it they were both telling the truth. Just the same, anonymity is sacred, to a point. Typically, a culling process encourages those with the strongest compulsion to go further, in which case they'd hook up in off-room private chats to skip around who would be the first to divulge their innermost desires, those cravings that may not only beg the issue of normalcy but would certainly lead to societal shunning were they exposed. But the very purpose of them being there was to anonymously express their secrets. That was the high. If the private chat proved fruitful, Skype with video might be next, and then a flesh and blood meeting if that went well. The three teenage girls that Adamson slashed had a gothic bent unbeknownst to their parents. They had been chat room regulars. The survivor went by Mrs. Drac, a married ruse to deflect any question of her being a minor but telegraphed the opposite in the process.

Adamson's MO was to chat up the females. When he felt certain he found one that might be faking her age he would confess that he was only 16 to encourage her to own up and do the same. Three quarters of the time he was right. When it appeared he was wrong they went their separate ways. Ratting out a minor on an S&M web site is wishful thinking. Secrecy is their common bond regardless of age. Just the same women scared him. Girls he could handle.

To put his victims' minds at ease, over the course of several weeks Adamson had arranged in-person meetings with each at a very public place with crowds about, without a Skype pre-screening under the pretext of a broken cam. Fifteen minutes after the appointed hour he walked up to each and in his guileless manner asked the time. Each was expecting a teenage boy and answered the odd looking, effeminate man not suspecting he was the one they were supposed to meet. "You look like you're waiting for someone," he said each time. "A friend," was more or less the safe answer each gave. "I hope your friend isn't coming on route 5." He then informed each there had been an accident on the freeway: "Backed up for hours." The disappointed girls went back home, never checked to see if there had been an accident, as he expected.

In spite of the initial no-show, getting the girls to meet a second time in a secluded location was easy, as though the first meeting actually took place. After all he was the one who had first suggested a safe harbor to break the ice. But all that's history. Two were dead and with the third still alive, though in a coma, time wasn't on his side and he knew it. Now that he'd used the three up he needed something more, fast.

Witch Woman signed into the chatroom about the same time as Killer13.

Janice Goldman had as many ideas as Max. She and preoccupied Lou Pasquale were seated in an Italian restaurant, Janice sipping the last of very good after-dinner Vin Santo to celebrate the three week anniversary of their first sex. She had been trying all night to grab his attention but he kept slipping back to the killings of the girls and, even more often, to Susan Stanich.

"Hmmm, wine's delicious," she said. "Like it?.....I said do you like the wine? Hey, Pasquale, I'm lonely...Pasquale, c'mere, join us."

"I'm, here, I'm here."

"Detective, you are somewhere else. Do you like the wine?"

"Yeah, it's great."

"Really? Don't you think you should taste it first to find out? Where are you this time?"

"Those girls," said Lou. "He's still out there and he'll do it again, I know it. Stanich says she can feel him, his energy. Maybe she can help us catch him. I just don't know. There's something more than strange about her. Everything she says seems to makes sense but she breaks the law all over the place and slips through our fingers at the same time. We got nothing on her but I'm afraid not to have her input. She knows things. Maybe she can save a life. I don't know."

"Flying through the air makes sense to you?"

"Yeah, it kinda does. They all say the same thing about her. It can't be a coincidence. It can't."

"She doesn't fly. Something else is going on. What does she say?"

"She says it's all in their mind. Maybe she's telling the truth. Maybe they all are. Insists she gets into their minds."

"Like she's gotten into yours?"

"She said the same thing."

"C'mon, we're getting out of here. You're taking us somewhere. It'll be a surprise. Let me have your wine. You're not drinking it."

"Where are we going?"

"If I told you then it wouldn't be a surprise, but it's guaranteed to take your mind off that woman. I promise. Think small."

"Great. I need the break," said Pasquale.

"The only woman you should have on your mind is me. This'll fix that. I want to meet this woman."

Dr. Goldman was maxed out on the two glasses of wine and deferred the driving to Lou. She was, however, in full stride when it came to giving directions. She opted for the circular route so they could enjoy the night air.

After half an hour Pasquale said, "We're going in circles."

"We're spiraling down to throw you off and give me time to study your handsome face." Pasquale couldn't help but puff up and enjoy the ride, the remainder of which was in silence except when Janice provided additional rights and lefts, mostly lefts. Ten minutes later they found themselves in the parking lot of the Valley River Medical Center where, coincidentally, Dr. Goldman had her office.

But that has nothing to do with why they were there. The doctor had something else in mind.

Janice led a puzzled Pasquale into the elevator where they rode up to the maternity floor, walked past the nurse's station and rooms of the new mothers until they came upon the large nursery windows. Janice pointed to the infants.

"Look Lou, Babies. Babies Lou." Lou was hypnotized.

"I adore babies," he said.

"I know," said Janice. "Me too. They're so new and smell good."

Detective Lou Pasquale's eyes went from one bassinette to the next, mesmerized. Janice's arrow hit its mark, straight into his Achilles heel. Without speaking a word they stayed in front of the nursery enjoying the unbounded optimism and limitless futures squirming, gurgling or sleeping to their delight. Then they walked back past the rooms and took the elevator down to the main floor, and walked out of the hospital. When they got to the car Janice said, "Are you ready to make a baby with me?"

"I'm ready," said Lou.

"Great," said Janice, and began unbuttoning her blouse. "Open the door for me please." For the next hour Lou Pasquale completely forgot about the investigation and the Stanich woman as he and Janice began the process that would eventually result in the conception of a baby boy who would one day look just like a beautiful little Pasquale. The back seat of the car was very romantic.

The following day Janice decided they should become engaged, to which Pasquale agreed with heartfelt relief because he was then off the hook in trying to figure out how to get around his fear of rejection and ask her to marry him. Now that that was settled he went right back to obsessing about two murders and a crazy woman who got off on neutralizing perverts and seemed to take delight in terrorizing maniacs.

Chapter 11

While that was going on Susan Stanich was trying to sort out an uncomfortable sensation that was making her skin crawl. The forces that favored her always seemed to have purpose that she never questioned. Rather she let herself be directed by energy with a pull no stronger than the draw of magnetism on a compass needle, but equally compelling. There was little doubt in her mind that she was cruising punk chatrooms for a reason. Static pinpoints were licking at her skin and her brain was lit. She was close to something.

What one might consider normal exhibits a wide variety of expressions. Diversity works. But the outlets for many of those on the various sites were far outside that wide range, probably the result of some early trauma in much the same way that a deformed sapling might result in a misshapen tree. I doubt you or I would find many of their most extreme appetites exciting. The politically correct impulse to accept all erotic expressions as 'cool' didn't really work in the outermost wastelands of those incapable of arousal without play acting dark theater. Nevertheless, as long as no one gets hurt who cares. But this was not the case.

Regulars in the chatrooms usually stopped in the group session seeking familiar, kindred spirits to hook up with, or perhaps someone new with a comparable or complementary bent, usually broadcast by their screen name. From the group setting they would move into a private chat where there would be no audience that could inhibit their trip.

Though there could be hundreds of visitors on a site only a dozen or so would be visible on the group page, mostly newcomers. In addition there were those who had outworn their welcome with other members on the site and were relegated to lurking for unsuspecting novices.

George Adamson sat at a booth in a library's technology lab staring at the screen of the computer he hacked into under a pseudonym. The library was one of five that he had employed to arrange meetings with women he met through the sites he frequented. Over the course of the previous year he had practiced and rehearsed his "Do you have the time" game more than a dozen times before his internal pressure cooker overflowed into action. Killer13 spotted Witch Woman immediately and sent her a private message. The dance the witch Knife had been seeking began–

KILLER13: Are you really a witch or just a bitch?

WITCH WOMAN: Both. I cast spells. Do you kill?

KILLER13: As a matter of fact I do. Would you like to die?

Susan Stanich immediately knew that she had just found the killer. Just like that.

WITCH WOMAN: I've thought about it. Life sucks.

KILLER13: Not if you make it interesting. You should make your life interesting.

WITCH WOMAN: Yeah, how would I do that?

KILLER13: A woman like you – you are a female aren't you?

WITCH WOMAN: Yes.

KILLER13: You have to let go. It can be very interesting. Just do it.

WITCH WOMAN: I don't do anything.

KILLER13: You should. You should do lots. It feels good, very good. Do you ever think about that?

WITCH WOMAN: Sure.

KILLER13: You like that, don't you? That's why you're here, isn't it?

WITCH WOMAN: I have to get off now. Sorry.

Susan Stanich abruptly closed out the connection, scheming to make him wonder why. Maybe she could be married. Or perhaps she was a kid and one of her parents or a sibling showed up. The latter possibility was the bait she was dangling. Thus she began reeling him in. And Adamson bit.

The chatroom was the only way Mrs. Stanich had been given to pinpoint the killer. The universe led her there but that was all she had to work with. The constant bombardment of energy she experienced hadn't separated him out from other negativity that fell upon her. So, like Pasquale and Millman she would have to do her own detective work to catch him. What set her apart from them was what she would do if she found him first.

Adamson sat in front of the computer monitor for several minutes. The emotional feelers of the insane are narrowly focused, often resulting in very heightened but limited perceptions. Having been through his vetting scenario many times before he felt that there was something very peculiar about what had just taken place. Little red flags were waving at him.

Millman applied a completely different line of methodology to detective work than Pasquale. Whereas Lou was partially fixated with relying on a hunch attack or the Stanich woman's intuition, or maybe crossing his fingers in the hope that a smoking gun would materialize to help catch the killer, Millman favored the textbook approach. This is why they make a great team, each filling in the spaces in the other's discovery technique to help create a complete picture. In the end they would both serve a just outcome, though not in this case.

Hackneyed clichés with obvious holes in them sometimes pay off. In this case Millman's assumption was that the murderer would return to the scene of the crime, kind of. Millman had police photographers sent to the funerals of the victims with the charge to discretely capture images of everyone who attended the services. The photos were them compared side-by-side to identity individuals who had attended both funerals. Due to the publicity surrounding the murders there were quite a few matches, mostly sensation seekers, crime groupies and the media. Women were eliminated and set aside just in case, known news personalities as well. When the screening was complete Detective Millman had a dozen or so persons of interest. But identifying them remained a problem. You can't broadcast images of a dozen men as suspects in murders based on a blind hunch. Besides lives being ruined there are laws that prohibit speculative policing without probable cause. He was stuck with clues he couldn't follow. One of the matches however caught his eye, a youngish man with sunglasses, wearing a hat. A scarf around his neck sufficiently blocked his face to the extent that he wasn't recognizable. What struck the detective was that he wore identical attire at both services and stood in the exact same place relative to the remainder of the mourning crowd. Millman's skin began to crawl. He was sure he was on to something but had no way to pursue the lead. “Shit,” he said.

Millman was sitting at his desk staring at 8” x 10” blow-ups of the man when Susan Stanich walked in.

“Where’s your partner?” she said. “He asked me to meet him at one.” Susan looked at her watch; “It’s one.”

“Shopping for an engagement ring. Give him five minutes. Probably got sidelined by a toddler. Were there any kids in front of the station house?”

“Yeah, a little girl in a stroller.”

“Oh, better give him 10 in case he spots her. I think we have something here,” said Millman pointing to the enlargements on his desk.

Susan walked over to his desk and looked at the images and began quivering. The witch Knife took over her being in the instant. “Dat’s him, dat’s da scumbag.”

“Just like that,” said Millman.

“Jus like dat.”

Millman’s hairs stood on end. He was transfixed by the transformation. She had changed in front of his eyes yet the same woman was standing before him, hunched over the pictures like a predator about to climb into the images to tear the man apart. In his gut he knew she was right. She just knew and now he was suspecting that his partner wasn’t all that crazy about the things he was saying about her. “Jesus,” he said, “who are you?”

“What is more like it,” she replied and just as quickly became Susan Stanich again.

In case you’ve been wondering what happened to Jack Stanich, he’s around, low profile yet always in the loop. We did mention that he shows up from time to time when he's needed. Other than that he remains on the sidelines and watches his favorite program, his family. He noticed that Max and Sunday March stopped their whispering when he walked within hearing and immediately knew something was going on that he wouldn't approve. He was needed.

"Okay, what is it," he said to Max. "If you tell me 'nothing' I'll get your mother and she'll pull it out of you, slowly and painfully. You're better off with me. What is it?"

Max knew she would figure it out in a minute and crash his brilliant plan. So he tap danced with a half truth side-step: "Sunday and I are going to the mall in Burlington, taking our bikes and the bus. We were going to tell you." Not a lie so far.

"You mean ask, right."

"Yeah, ask, that's what I meant."

"Just the two of you? What's wrong with the mall in Bellingham?"

"Boring....just the two of us. Yep."

"No way. Patricia's going with you...PATRICIA..."

"Oh no," said Max.

"Oh yep," said Jack. And that was that.

Two hours later the three of them were in Burlington stuck at the mall with Max trying to figure out how to get rid of Patricia. The forces about were laughing their heads off as they sucked out every wily ploy that popped into Max's head and threw each into the wind. He suggested shopping, the latest chick flick, even boy watching, which made her wince at his invasion of a very personal space.

"Okay, we're not here for the mall. What's going on?" said Patricia.

"Okay, okay...but you have to promise not to divulge what you're about to see."

"I'll decide that after I find out what you're up to."

The three of them headed to the off-track betting parlor. When they got there Max slipped inside and grabbed a racing sheet before he was thrown out, then they hung across the street watching the flow of walk-in traffic, then Max and his sister took position where he could intercept a likely candidate, one who looked respectable, trustworthy. At a betting parlor that would be a stretch but he would give it a try. Sunday remained across the street with the camera on his phone, discretely in hand, aimed at the action. When the mark walked by Max said, "I'd put my money on 'Fast Track' in the fourth if I were you. The mark looked at the Stanich kids, chuckled and walked past them into the parlor. Ten minutes later he came out looking for them. Though Max started out as a Cassandra he quickly became an oracle.

"No thank yous," Max said to the mark. He handed the man a bill. "Put this $20 on Homeward Bound in the 6th. It's a 30 to 1 long shot. You can bet what you want. None of our business." The man looked around and put the $20 in his pocket. "When you come out you'll give us $600 and that'll be it. If you leave with our money...my friend across the street, who took a picture of you taking money from a kid in front of a betting parlor, will send the picture to the police and then post it on the internet."

"How do I know you won't send the picture anyway?"

"You don't but we won't," said Max."That's the deal, take it or leave it and give me the $20 back and walk. All bets will be off, including the one you were going to make." Ethics, morality or possible consequences don't stand a chance against a long-shot sure thing.

Fifteen minutes later Max, Patricia and Sunday March were heading back to the bus terminal with smiles on their faces and $600 in their pockets. Patricia clearly saw the wisdom in keeping close mouthed. Thereafter the trio would become an inseparable team several days that week. Max was the visionary while Sunday March brought the PhD in street smarts he'd earned in orphanages. Patricia contributed adult supervision that was ignored. Jack was delighted that the kids were bonding. He was sincerely touched. And Mrs. Stanich was too preoccupied with serious to smell the rats.

Susan Stanich was with Pasquale and Millman when Alice Summers called. The Stanich house shared one cell phone staged near the front door that the kids could take and replace when they went out, an added security thing for their safety and Susan's peace-of-mind. She rarely used it but carried it on her person when extraordinary circumstances seemed to make it the sensible thing to do. Since the murders she kept it with her and had given the number to the detectives. Millman then gave it to Alice's mother to calm her anxiety, and she passed the number to Alice who was calling Susan to organize theatrics for her dramatic escape, which she figured should feature prime time television coverage and a heart wrenching reunion with her mother. To lend a tone of authenticity in preparation for the call Alice did deep knee bends until she was breathless.

"Who is this? said Susan.

"Hi," gasped Alice. "This is Alice Summers, the kidnapped girl everyone's looking for."

"Who told you that?"

"Told me what?"

"Who told you everyone's looking for you? I'm not. What do you want?"

"I want to arrange my release from captivity."

"Okay, arrange it," said Susan and hung up.

A panting Alice Summers sat on the leather couch, naked, stunned. The kidnapper was pacing the floor.

"Don't tell me they won't even take you back now," he said. "What am I supposed to do with you? Can't you just leave?"

"You fucking idiot," screamed Alice. "You kept me too long."

"I've been trying to get rid of you for 5 weeks. Who has the keys to the car? You do? This is really really fucked.," he said.

"Why don't you leave?" said Alice.

"I can't. I just can't." The poor kidnapper was so infatuated he was like a monkey trying to get an apple out of a bottle when the hand was too big to get out of the bottle and hold the apple at the same time. He was stuck.

"Shit," said Alice. "I may as well get dressed. I bet you don't even want me now, do you?"

"I wouldn't go that far but you've definitely lost your cachet. Maybe it's just as well. Our kid would probably have been an idiot like you."

"What do we do now?"

"You're the one who screwed everything up. You figure it out. Start by getting dressed."

"I'll get dressed when you take off that stupid mask."

"Fuck you."

"Fuck you back and double."

Children shouldn't have children.

"That'll fix the little bitch," said Susan and began laughing her head off, soon joined by Millman and Pasquale, neither of whom were really sure why they laughing, a contagious thing. When things subsided the absurdity of Alice's kidnapping lingered. Pasquale asked, "How could you be so sure she was never in any danger?"

"I don't know. It pops into my head just like I know our killer is ramping up for more. But we don't have time for Summers now. I'll catch up with her and her friend later."

"And the killer," said Millman.

"I'm going to flush him out. But we capture, don't kill. That's the deal."

"Can't promise that," said Pasquale.

"Not asking for promises. That's the deal, the only deal. This guy's in pain, very damaged. You can't go in thinking to put him down. We're here to stop the killing and put him in a place where he can live out his miserable life. He didn't ask to be crazy when he was born. It's not his fault. You don't like it, go it alone. I'll do the same. No hard feelings."

"We're cops not philosophers," said Millman.

"That's why I'm here, help you see another way of looking at things. This ain't white collar greed so forget rational motives. There's no logical explanation for why violent criminals do what they do. Killers are killers long before they kill, incubating, already programmed. The circumstances that trigger their crimes are just catalysts, what we call motives, but the real causes are ancient crazy stuff along a path probably molded by a genetic defect or bad childhoods they didn't ask for. Our job is to stop them, not punish them. And you can forget rehabilitation while you're at it. Rarely works and certainly not as a result of any well-meaning, imaginary epiphany behind bars, which is why most end up recidivists. Fellas, they see themselves as damaged goods and feel more comfortable with like-minded cons than upwardly mobile whitebread. To criminals, jail is more than a hotel, it's home. I know all about it and you never will. We stop him, don't hurt him. Non-negotiable. You in?"

"Suppose we have no choice and he forces the issue," said Pasquale.

"Won't happen. That's my end of the deal."

"I can't wait to see how you do this," said Millman.

"Yeah, well, you won't. I'm gonna whisper in his ear and you'll never hear a thing."

The next day the surviving victim from the slashings was slowly being brought out of an induced coma. The girl's return to consciousness was kept from the media so as not to drive the killer underground. When the doctors felt it appropriate, Pasquale and Millman were allowed ten minutes to question her. Still unable to speak from the wounds to her throat, she answered their questions with pad and pen, providing enough of a physical description and the web site where she met the killer to confirm Millman's hunch and Stanich's intuition. But the girl was still too disoriented to pinpoint the times of her online contacts with the killer, which may have helped narrow down the search. Knowing which meeting ground was helpful but tracking and weeding the hundreds of internet addicts frequenting the chatroom in the days leading up to the attack could take months.

Susan Stanich was way ahead of the detectives and there was no way she would let them know. She works alone, like she told them. While they were at the hospital she was chatting again with Killer13. They'd hooked up on the group page. From there he sent her a private message.

KILLER13: Wow, you're back

WITCH WOMAN: Here I be

KILLER13: I was hoping you'd show up

WITCH WOMAN: Been around a few times.

KILLER13: Were you looking for me?

WITCH WOMAN: Rather not say.

KILLER13: Have you been thinking about what we said?

WITCH WOMAN: Maybe

KILLER13: I think about this stuff all the time

WITCH WOMAN: Figures

KILLER13: You're teasing me

WITCH WOMAN: That's why I'm here

KILLER13: Maybe we can meet somewhere and you can tease me all you want

WITCH WOMAN: Not a good idea. I don't know you

KILLER13: I don't know you either. Maybe you're a crazy woman

WITCH WOMAN: Nope, just a witch

KILLER13: It can be a place where we both feel safe, maybe a mall. But I don't always have a car.

WITCH WOMAN: I'm thinking about it. How come no car?

KILLER13: If I tell you will you still chat with me?

WITCH WOMAN: You have to tell me first

KILLER13: I'm 16. My parents don't always let me have the car

On the occasions he'd guessed wrong and found himself with an adult, the other party invariably broke the connection fast fearing a possible entrapment. He waited to see if she would respond. Susan let it hang a few beats. Part of her MO is teasing, just like she said.

WITCH WOMAN: Wow, we're perverts. I'm only 15

KILLER13: How fun

WITCH WOMAN: Gotta go...

Over the following 72 hours Susan would keep reeling him in, tighter and tighter, exchanging tales of leather and piercing fantasies, matching tattoos the two of them might someday get, when they had enough money, and their parent's permission. Both claimed groupie fixations with the Gothic Rock/Darkwave music scene. Susan expected that, didn't take ESP. She confessed a devotion to Adele though that great voice wasn't in the script she had planned on following. Susan tells everyone, couldn't help herself; she's Adele's biggest fan. Besides, that sidestep provided an air of authenticity.

While Stanich was playing George Adamson, George Adamson was pinging her with an IP geo application that gave him her exact location. Susan Stanich, on the other hand, would never rely on crude technology for her information.

Chapter 12

At the same time, the surviving victim's laptop was on its way to the police tech lab where the hard drive could reveal digital ghosts from the web site where the girl had been, maybe when, possibly with whom. Millman personally drove and then walked the drive to the lab, talking on his cell with Pasquale every step of the way as though constant contact between the partners would speed things along. Once the chatroom meeting ground had been revealed by the survivor, computers from the other two victims were obtained from relatives and also on their way to the lab.

It was in Pasquale's competitive nature, he couldn't help himself. The omnipresent danger presented by a killer on the loose was in the forefront of his mind, but pressing not far behind was his detective's drive to eclipse the Stanich woman in finding the perp. He'd called Janice Goldman and cancelled their dinner date, again, the third evening in a row. Technically it was only two because she had been summoned to the hospital to help deliver an early term breech birth and wouldn't have been able to make it anyway. She didn't let Pasquale know that, so he remained on the hook for three.

Within hours police tech specialists uncovered some of the secrets buried on the drive, unveiling IP addresses that were then traced to PCs at three library computer labs. Each PC had been used to contact the girl in the days prior to the murders. The exercise quickly provided the name, sex and age of more than 100 visitors to the library's labs. Women and males under 20 were eliminated by virtue of educated guess and expediency. That left 43 males. Millman's speculation was that only 42 had used their real names and addresses. Plus they had video from the security cameras stationed at the entrances to the libraries to complete the tools needed for a process of elimination.

Pasquale then fielded the task force assigned the case, pairs of detectives armed with cameras and profiles of the suspect. They were instructed to confirm the identification of the names they were given. Provided they didn't stumble upon the killer, each individual was to be questioned and then, with permission, photographed. The MO was that they would purge all but the suspect. Both Pasquale and Millman felt certain he went under a pseudonym. He wouldn't exist; phony name, fake address. The photos the task force took would then be compared to the images captured by the libraries' security cameras. When only one possibility remained, he would have to be their man. That individual's photo would then be compared to the suspect culled from the funerals' images. The methodology occupied the better part of two days and nights and it worked but it didn't help. The killer walked in each library wearing a capped hat, head down, and then hacked into a web site forbidden on library computers using an alias. What Pasquale didn't know was that in the months prior the killer had visited each library and made mental note of the camera locations. In those preceding months he was just one of nondescript thousands who had visited the libraries. All in all Millman's hunch was a smart move, like having photos taken at the funerals, but another dead end. Meticulous detective work can be tedious and laborious and still not pan out. Even reading about hunch-work can be a drag. Pasquale and Millman were trying but Susan Stanich was way ahead of them. And now she decided it was time to bring Patricia in.

After several days of stringing him along Susan felt the killer was ripe so she took Patricia out to lunch under the pretext of quality mother/daughter time. However, the two of them never went to a restaurant without the rest of the household. The girl's antennae went up. She was sure their investment project was on the table and she, being the eldest, would take the fall. Naturally enough, Max and Sunday also felt certain the unusual girl-time had to do with their venture and appropriately enough became paranoid about Patricia spilling the beans. They had nothing to worry about. Patricia, on the other hand, did.

Susan needed bait she could trust. Asking a friend or neighbor to borrow a daughter to catch a killer would have been a bit much, hence Patricia. Besides, they'd worked together on a similar project years before even if Patricia's memory of such was a blank.

"It was Max's idea," blurted Patricia, menu in hand, as soon as they were seated.

"What was Max's idea?"

"You know."

"No, I don't."

"In that case I'm getting a tuna fish sandwich and fries."

"No fries," said her mother. "What is Max up to?"

"He'll kill me. You ask him yourself."

"Is it dangerous?"

"Not really...no, it's not dangerous. It's funny but let him tell you."

Susan Stanich gave her daughter a long hard stare. Patricia eyes revealed only feckless innocence so she let the matter lie and got down to business. “There’s another Eloise DeMarco on the loose. Fun time is over.”

“What do you want me to do?”

“You and I are going to catch him.”

“Mom, you’re crazy.”

“Nobody’s perfect.”

Once George Adamson felt secure that Witch Woman was the likely candidate who could provide release from his agony, the floodgate of black energy from the reservoir in his dark soul began to flow. Anticipation rippled through his body and burst from every pore raining upon the universe, a violent eruption intent on expression. Animals and birds sensed the oncoming storm, and so too did the witch.

In his bones Adamson suspected he was coming to the end of a journey as though his life force was escaping and he would evaporate from the world with no one knowing or caring. A profound sadness enveloped the poor deranged man-child. There was only one place he wanted to be; home, not that he had one.

The immaculately kept, tree-lined driveway to the walled compound was a quarter mile long, a flawless picture in the crisp afternoon. Adamson parked his car near the entrance, unconcerned that his parents could see it there. After all they had no idea the make of his car. They didn’t even know what he looked like, hadn’t seen him since he was a child more than twenty years prior. He could walk up to either and ask directions and they would have no idea who he was. But he wanted to see them, not that he would confront them, still terrified of the certain rejection that would only add to the weight of pain upon him. Staking out the driveway to catch sight of his mother or father was a long shot unlikely to bear fruit. He knew that but felt compelled to go through the paces, like his fantasy that his mother would one day show up and claim him.

As he paced up and back on the grassy sloped side of the country road early memories of abandonment revisited him with stinging clarity. He was a lonely child again being lectured on his parents' need for isolation, to be free from the burdens of child rearing. As he looked down the long driveway at the massive house at the end he vividly recalled all the times he was told there was no room for him there. He stood on the side of the road, again that little boy, and cried as he had never cried in his life for his loneliness.

Occasionally cars passed. He turned his face from each, wanting no one to see his tears, certain they wouldn't care one way or the other. Just the same he didn't want confirmation of his invisibility. No more pain, no more hurt. His tears ran out yet he still stood for hours in the fading afternoon and waited. Then off in the distance he could see a limousine approaching. He knew it was them, chauffeured as always. He quickly fixed on the car not caring if they saw him watching. He desperately wanted to see his parents who had hurt him so deeply. And he did. They passed within several feet of him and he could see perfectly his mother and father, she being the closer. As a child he had never seen them this close. They were much older than he remembered but their countenance hadn't changed. The imperious distance and visible annoyance at having to look upon another of a lesser class remained on her face as she coldly glanced at him and then away in irritation at having been exposed to his existence. His father's eyes were locked straight ahead, having no more need to look upon him than he would a servant. He wondered if they remembered that they had fathered him at all. And then there was only the back of the car moving down the gravel driveway through the avenue of trees framing the road. He wanted to kill someone. So he returned to his luxury condo and got back on the computer.

Now for a harebrained intermission, just like in real life: Wacky, beautiful Alice Summers was enraged. She'd called the police and asked the status of the Alice Summers case and was told she had been downgraded to a runaway. She wasn't even kidnapped anymore. Alice was so angry she got dressed even though the kidnapper still refused to take off his mask. And he, on his part, felt so bad he went out that night and bought her an engagement ring. Upon returning he went directly to his knees.

"What the fuck are you doing down there?" said Alice.

"Will you marry me?" said her former kidnapper.

"I'm 16 years old you moron. I don't love you. I don't even know what you look like. I don't like you and I'm not pregnant. Why in the world would I marry you? Give me one good reason. Me, marry an idiot? That'll be the day."

"But I love you," he said.

"'But I love you?' That's why I should marry you, because 'But I love you?' That's the reason? I feel like I'm talking to a parking meter. You don't love me anymore than you loved the five others before me."

"I loved them."

"No, you didn't. You seduced them and fucked them, forbidden fruit and all that. They were only kids and they didn't scare you. You don't want me. You want what you can't have. In this case it happens to be me. You're just a male. You're all like that, leeches until you score, dogs. Let's talk about that ring. Let me see it."

"No marriage, no ring."

"Gimme the dammed ring," she said and snatched it from him and looked it over. "I'll keep the diamond. You can wear the ring yourself. Let's take it apart and then I'm going home."

"No way. You can't just leave me," he said.

"Oh, so now you're back to being a kidnapper. Is that it? Okay, here's your extra set of fucking car keys back," and she threw them at him. "I'll lock the door. Which side do you want to be on? Locked in or locked out? Moron. This is all your fault. After this is over I never want to see you again, ever. Come to think of it I haven't seen you in the first place. Take off that idiotic mask."

And he did.

"Wow," she said," you're not a bad looking man for your age. Not bad looking at all. You know you didn't have to go through all this crap just to get laid."

"That's not it."

"Then why."

"I don't know. It was just a dumb idea that kind of snowballed. The first one was like a game. That was Cynthia. Told me she was 19. Most of it was her idea. She got pregnant and made up this whole story so her parents wouldn't kill her and to keep me out of jail. Then she went to my crazy mother. One lie led to another. I didn't hurt anyone, not ever, always tried to put the parents' mind at ease...the girls eventually wanted a baby. I know, it sounds crazy."

"You couldn't hurt a fly but the cops think you're some kind of psycho. You're just a silly dumb mama's boy. You'll have to go to jail. You know that don't you?"

"I know. Will you visit me?"

"Sure, as soon as I set up live television coverage of my dramatic escape and your capture. We need an angle."

"How 'bout 'We fell in love and now I want to go straight so we can be together one day?'"

"No one will believe I'm that stupid."

Think of this tale as alternating slices of the idiocy life offers up, an interesting swirl of unfortunate, extreme drama sandwiched by weightless comedy. The narrator suspects the purpose of life, if there is one, leans toward the latter. That's why we have to work so hard at serious, going over, under and around the residue from our damage. Funny, on the other hand, flows naturally, easy, like Max and Sunday March, a lighthearted pair of pissers grinning through their days. Maybe nothing fazes them because they know the secret ingredient; absurdity. Just the same there is one person who can give them pause; their mother.

"Max, sweetheart, come here," said Susan. "Come sit by me. Let's talk."

Susan never called Max sweetheart unless he was in deep shit. The nicer she was the worse it could be. Accordingly, things looked really bad. Max's strategy was to do the only thing possible, nothing; do nothing, say nothing. It wouldn't work.

"Max, honey, what is it that Patricia won't tell me? She said I should ask you. Hmm, hon, what are you up to? Tell mom. I won't hit. Promise. C'mere." Max slowly walked over and sat down next to his mother, whereupon she gave him a good smack in the back of his neck. "That's an advance. If I don't get fast answers there'll be lots more," and she smacked him again.

Now, I know there are readers who may be offended by Susan's child rearing method employing corporal punishment. In her defense I suspect she might say she is merely following the example set by creatures in the animal kingdom who she feels are wiser about these things. It was an encouraging little whap; no karate chop. That she smacked Max in advance was wrong. Yes it was. And if Mrs. Stanich finds out that it wasn't justified she would own up to her mistake and owe her son something nice. See.

"Well, hon, got something to share with mom, huh?" said Susan.

"Patricia, Sunday and I –" and she cut him off.

"Please, keep them out of it and cut the crap," she said. "They may have gone along but I know who's at the bottom of whatever it is you came up with." And she whapped him once more because three's a charm.

"Okay, okay....stop that, okay. We're going into investment banking."

"Really? That takes money. You have no money."

"We had $10. And then we got lucky."

"Stop bullshitting me. I'm embarrassed for you. Try to just say it."

And so it was that Max informed his mother the source of the thirteen thousand dollars in cash that the three of them had accumulated in just four days.

"We did Anacortes twice, which was a mistake because there was a crowd outside waiting for us begging for a tip after we hit it big the second day in a row. We had to run to get away. Patricia's an idiot. She yelled out number three in the fourth when we took off. They'll kill us if we ever go back. They must have lost a fortune. Burlington we did just once but we plan on going back when it cools down. Everett's good, and if you can give us a ride we think Yakima would be even better. Mom, think expensive college education times three."

Susan Stanich sat and listened to the system Max came up with to be certain he was in no danger and the likelihood of getting caught minimal, which would lead to nothing anyway. Authorities would sooner believe he was in on some fix they couldn't prove than grasp that he could see into the future, a gift that passed Susan by. After a moment or two of pondering the plusses and minuses of the scheme she said, "Okay, we can use the money. Now what do you have in mind for stocks?"

During the morning briefing other members of the task force volunteered their opinions, which for the most part were against placing Susan Stanich under surveillance. Pasquale and Millman were going up and back on whether or not they should or could do it and how Susan Stanich might react if she discovered the tail. Pasquale couldn't confide in the crew the reason he thought she was on to something; they would have thought him nuts. Millman wasn't sure one way or the other because he had seen the woman do some strange things. In the end Pasquale's unexplained hunch won out and they assigned two detectives to guard or watch Susan Stanich, depending on your point of view. But no one thought to put a tail on Patricia.

By mid-morning two detectives sat in a car up the road from the Stanich house sipping cliché coffee, ready to follow the woman. What they didn't know is that they would never see her leave because she wasn't going anywhere. That's not how she does things. With his daughter alongside, Jack Stanich drove past the detectives and took his daughter to a mall.

A half hour later, Patricia was at the mall full of shoppers waiting for the killer. Jack Stanich had no idea what was up with his girls yet would definitely seize the opportunity to go window shopping for fishing tackle at two sporting goods stores. Susan was laying on her bed seeking a sign of some kind that might warn her of impending danger though she was fairly confident Patricia would be fine in a crowd. However, a barber's razor was gripped in her hand, the same one she'd carried her entire life, a memento from life on the streets of Manhattan.

Susan was incapable of pinpointing the pain-filled energy from George Adamson, his malevolent force no more than a black tree in a dark forest. Yet Susan was keenly attuned to the vibrations from her daughter, which is how she located her child when Patricia had been kidnapped years before. The waves emanating from Patricia's spirit remained clean. As such she had little concern for her daughter's safety.

Susan had obtained photo prints of the suspect's images taken at the funerals and did the same with digital captures from the libraries' security cameras. Though there was no definitive shot of his face, the images gave the Stanich women enough to be reasonably confident they could recognize their man if he showed up. The surviving victim provided the killer's pattern, which was confirmed by

Susan when Killer13 suggested they meet in a safe place. She knew this exercise would only be his trial run. The real event was yet to come.

Susan had to catch him in the act. As she saw it that was the only way he couldn't slip through a loophole in the law. There were no fingerprints or clues, nothing. What little they had would be circumstantial because the survivor never saw his face. The media was on to the S&M chatroom connection and warnings were broadcast that were not only ignored but actually resulted in increased traffic to the S&M sites, such is human nature. Though events were moving quickly Stanich wanted to speed things along even faster, before the killer disappeared in case the snowballing limelight proved too bright.

As long as she was surrounded by a throng of people Patricia felt safe enough to relish the intrigue, a case of acute junior detective; think Sherley Holmes. Not wanting to miss a thing, she showed up in front of the agreed upon shoe outlet fifteen minutes ahead of the appointed time in case the killer did the same, which he did but outside of her imagination Patricia didn't know that. From a pizza store across the mall aisle George Adamson watched her talking incessantly on a phone. What he didn't know was that there was no one on the other end of the line. The phone was to her ear but her finger was on the video feature. Nevertheless, his picture in the hands of police might only pause his rampage. Stopping him was the objective.

For half an hour Patricia patiently stood or walked around pretending to be talking on her cell. At almost the precise time her mother predicted he showed up, fifteen minutes late. She got a full face on video of him as he walked up to her and asked the time just as her mother said he would. Patricia was taken a bit aback at the ethereal, pink man before her. He looked so different, and sad and lonely. Under other circumstances she could see him asking the time if only for a momentary contact with another human. Half of her felt sorry for him. The other half was terrified.

Susan could feel the waves of her daughter's adrenaline and grasped the folded barber's razor tightly in her hand, flipping it open and closed, a nervous tic from her childhood when danger was present, a reflex from the years when she was the angry teenage prostitute Knife. The creature within Susan was crouched, ready to pounce.

George Adamson hated what he saw, a pretty, vivacious, happy girl, easy prey to balance the perpetual agony he suffered if only for a moment. He would do anything for that brief reprieve; kill as he had before. It's not love of money but jealousy and envy that are nearest the root of all evil. Love of money is a symptom just as jealousy and envy are the after effects. The real root causes will be found hidden in the span of time measured from the beginning of a being's existence, starting in the womb. Along the way the soul can be twisted into a kaleidoscope of deviations from the norm, like George Adamson when his parents buried him alive. Child abuse is the root of all evil.

Adamson also liked what he saw. If this was to be the end of his spree, Patricia Stanich would be his perfect swan song.

Patricia, incapable of following her mother's precise instructions, got caught up in the subterfuge and began to ad lib. The rush from danger can be addictive. For the moment she was hooked. Instead of saying thanks and going on her way when informed the interstate was blocked, she engaged the baby-faced killer "Where on the interstate is the accident?"

"I thought I heard it was to the north, maybe Ferndale. Not sure."

"Oh, you didn't see it," she said.

"No, I came from Mt. Vernon," he said.

"Isn't there a mall in Burlington? How come you came all the way here?"

"Sure...listen I'm late. Sorry, have go. Thanks for the time." He quickly walked off.

Patricia was left to come down from the adrenaline high on her own. When she got home Mrs. Stanich would help some. Patricia found her father in the fishing tackle section of the sporting goods store drooling over dry flies.

"Time to go?" said Jack.

"No rush," said Patricia. She knew her mother would pull every detail of the encounter out of her. She figured her mother's fury would follow shortly thereafter. "Nope, take your time."

Susan would have no reason to be angry. Patricia's little improv sent up more red flags. George Adamson's heightened state told him something wasn't quite what it appeared to be. Then it popped into his head; the girl had been expecting him. She wasn't the least surprised by his story of the traffic jam. They were on to him. And now he was on to them as well.

Susan Stanich smiled as she woke from sleep; Patricia was so predictable, a good kid.

Pasquale answered his cell on the second ring tone. "Do you actually think you could stake out my house and I wouldn't know it?" said Susan. There was a long silence while Pasquale was trying to decide whether a clever quip or feigned ignorance would suit the moment. "Lou baby, do you guys ever catch crooks or do you just scare them away?"

"Mrs. Stanich, put yourself in my place. What would you do?"

"The last thing I would do is irritate me if I thought I flew through the air. That would be a really big mistake, now wouldn't it? And if I'm just a regular, average run-of-the-mill non-witch then there would be no reason to stake out my house to begin with. In either case it makes no sense. Please send them home. Either that or have take-out delivered. I'm not feeding them." Jack and Patricia then walked in the front door. Susan hung up the phone and moved her irritation from Pasquale to her daughter who was now the recipient of a killer stare.

"Moron," said Susan, feigning anger. "Now, every word and let me see what we're dealing with. Patricia handed her the cell phone and Susan looked over the video of him while her daughter dutifully reported every breath he took.

To speed things along Susan Stanich gave the killer an extra hour before going back to the chatroom. The slower her response the quicker he would rush the pace. Of course he was there, anxiously waiting, ripe for the picking. And she stuck it to him.

KILLER13: hey

WITCH WOMAN: hey? where were you? I waited an hour

KILLER13: Must've just missed you. an accident on 5

WITCH WOMAN: yeah sure

KILLER13: I swear

WITCH WOMAN: just kidding...some creepy guy told me

KILLER13: (long pause) Why was he creepy

WITCH WOMAN: I think he was hitting on me...made my skin crawl...looked like bubble gum...at least he didn't touch me...what a geek

KILLER13: That's mean

WITCH WOMAN: told you I was a bitch...but not his bitch

KILLER13: Can we try again

WITCH WOMAN: what do you have in mind

Chapter 13

Max and Sunday March were on their own. This resulted in an unfortunate, unforeseen turn of events unless you were with them on the laughing side of the dingy green precinct desk. At the precise moment that Susan was setting up George Adamson for his permanent, all-expenses-paid vacation or execution, the choice would be his; the boys were sitting in the interrogation room of a police station being questioned by very confused cops.

Gamblers who frequent off-track betting location are emotionally connected to all others of a like addiction. And gamblers, like family, talk. They talk about the time they hit a trifecta, or about the day after when they blew the wad on a hot tip that turned cold when the jockey was thrown or the quarterback got sacked. The highlights of each and every major win or loss since the beginning of time are served up again and again for endless, obsessive speculation on the infinite manifestations of lady luck, about which gamblers never tire. Gaps in this non-stop narrative of 'what ifs' will be laced with hard, factual, scientific superstition, the kind of stuff gamblers come up with to explain their next fail/safe system to manipulate random chance, especially when it's in favor of the house.

Every nickel that falls a gambler's way will become a loss sooner or later because gamblers play to lose. That's the objective. Even if a gambler momentarily hits, h/she will then double down and lose it all. Losing is inevitable.

Without losing there would be no gambling, only investing and spending would be left. So, when Max and Sunday March showed up the whole purpose of gambling got screwed up and the gamblers won, and they talked. And the boys got caught. And they couldn't stop laughing.

Max decided to tell the cops the absolute truth. That's how the giggles got started. "I can predict which horse is gonna win cause I can see into the future, but only sometimes. For example I have no idea what you're going to do with me next." He and Sunday March then went into uncontrollable fits of laughter.

"Okay. Who's feeding you the tips? We know the races are rigged. Who's behind it," said interrogator number one.

Max appeared to give it serious thought and then offered up: "God?"

"You know what we're looking for. Who is it?" insisted number two. There was no good guy bad guy because both were quite nice. The affable Max and Sunday March team could charm anyone.

"You wanna know who's gonna win tomorrow at Emerald Downs in the fourth? Yes?" said Sunday, offering up Max's special talent. "Gimme a twenty and I'll place it for you."

"Don't listen to him," said Max. "If you do you'll lose your money."

"Suppose he's right," said number one.

"He can't be right," said Max.

"Yeah, why not?"

"Because there's no racing tomorrow at Emerald Downs. Why don't you just give me your money and we'll call it even." It took a full five minutes before the boys could control their hysteria. Not much later Jack showed up to take Max and Sunday home. He sat with them briefly to hear their side of the story and then he too began laughing.

"What are the charges?" he asked the police Lt. overseeing the questioning. "Show me one witness who will confess to taking a tip from a 12-year-old. Can you prove my boys placed even one bet? Did they lie to anyone about their ages? Did they do anything illegal? Well? No? Okay, we're leaving. You know where to reach us. C'mon," he said to the boys. "We gotta get home. Your mother wants me to drop Patricia off somewhere."

Just as they were about to leave Max whispered something to Jack and he turned to the officer in charge, "Excuse me but don't you think you should return their money?" Number one handed an envelope to Max. Only then did the three of them leave, with the boys $2,345 ahead for the day.

On the way to the car Jack said to his son, "Your mother wants me to pick up a copy of the New York Times on the way. Do you know what that's about?"

"Nope," said Max.

It seemed that half the police in the state of Washington were now following the escapades of the Stanich family. Susan hated the thought of having to move again but being in the spotlight made her skin crawl.

Lou Pasquale and Janice Goldman were trying to have a nice quiet dinner, but it was too quiet. Pasquale wasn't talking again because his mind was spinning, chock full of Stanich stuff. Janice was a reasonable person but when her man had another woman on his mind reason went out the window. He might shortly follow if she couldn't reel him in.

"I'm pregnant," said Janice. Pasquale didn't react and kept twirling his pasta, sort of making little neat piles, rearranging the food on his plate so that the heaps were all nice and even. "I said I'm pregnant," she repeated, much louder.

"You're pregnant?" said Pasquale

"Pasquale, how could I know if I'm pregnant? It's been only a few days since we started this project but that got your attention. Nothing else has worked. C'mon," she said. "I think it's best if we keep the momentum going," and dragged him into the bedroom. The dining room table would've worked too but they weren't that comfortable with one another quite yet. That familiarity would take at least another week.

Once work on the project was complete, Lou pillow talked. "You're not gonna believe this but her kid has had people placing bets for him in three cities and he wins every time. These are not normal people."

"No one's normal. That's just a hypothetical mid-point between regular people. Please...don't tell me you're back to thinking she flies through the air."

"I don't know anymore. I just don't know."

"I really have to meet this woman. Soon. Let's work on the project again."

"Please don't hang up," begged Alice Summers. As soon as Susan Stanich heard Alice's voice on her cell she felt worse than a blackboard being scratched. She wanted to pull her hair out. Fortunately the girl was out of reach.

"Where's your friend, the kidnapper?" said Susan.

"He's right here."

"Put that moron on."

"Hello," whispered the kidnapper in the half-hearted voice of a confessor owning up.

"What?" yelled Susan into the phone. "What did you say?"

"Hello."

"Hello. Hello. Is that the best you can do, you idiot? Hello? Why the fuck are you calling me?"

"I don't know," he said.

"You do realize I'm going to catch you and put that little dick of yours in jail. By the time you get out you'll either be gay or too old to use it. Moron. Put the prima donna back on."

"Hello," said Alice.

"What do you want?" said Susan.

"I wanted to tell you I know what he looks like."

"Oh, shit," said Susan and hung up.

"Now that was really bright," said the kidnapper.

"Shut up," said Alice. "We need a plan."

"No, we don't," said the kidnapper. "Just keep calling people and tell them how stupid you are."

"Why don't you just leave?" said Alice.

"Me leave? This is my place. You leave."

"I have no place to go," said Alice."

"Go home."

"I can't. My mother took back the red car offer and the performing arts school in Los Angeles. She said if I like it here so much maybe I should stay."

The following morning was showtime. Susan Stanich started off with her husband because he was the most reasonable and required the least amount of explanation. The others would have to be thrown in place.

"Patricia's biking over to Whatcom Falls Park in an hour or so."

"I thought I was driving her somewhere."

"I decided she should be able to handle this herself. I was hoping you wouldn't mind staying close to the boys and make sure they don't wander off."

"Where are you going to be?" said Jack.

"Right here, taking a nap." But the way she said it sent the hairs on Jack's neck stand on end. He'd seen and heard her like this before, many times, but it was the matter of degree that set this episode apart. In the past whatever she might have been up to she kept to herself and he would invariably skip alongside the incidents lightly. This wasn't one of those. The last time he'd seen her this focused yet completely distant from her surroundings was when their daughter had been kidnapped years before. One again she was scary and that made him nervous. He wasn't afraid for her, more likely afraid of her, though not for himself or the kids. Someone was about to meet up with a nightmare in the light of day and wide awake. Common myth holds that witches conduct their business only at night. That makes as much sense as concluding there are no stars in the sky during the day. Witches have no set hours and the energy from the heavens pours down upon us day and night.

Next came the Max & Sunday March team, whom she corralled and gathered around the kitchen table. "Go to the financial section of the Times. Research your intuition and bring me five good picks. Show me three long term investments; two others can be a bit on the risky side but no penny stock nonsense. I'm gonna ask you questions about dividends, performance, capitalization and management. Make sure you have the answers. If you skip anything I keep the money and spend it on clothes I don't want or need. Are we jake?"

"What does jake mean?"

"Find out. That's part of your assignment. Now get me the skinny on your picks. We'll discuss them when I get back."

"Where are you going?" said Sunday.

"I'm taking a nap."

Lastly, were the instructions to her daughter. The bond between them made certain communication unnecessary, like the importance of not deviating from her mother's instructions again, this time in a life and death situation. One look at Susan's blue-blue eyes was all it took. Stressing the critical nature of their 'project' would have been overkill.

"Take a knife just in case," she said, "the one I told you not to carry anymore. Keep your back against a large open space or a wall if there is one. Wait for him. Do not go looking. He'll be watching and find you. Keep your hand on that knife all the time. Just keep it in your hand. Got it?"

"Yes."

"Good."

"What's the plan?" Patricia asked.

"There is no plan. You just show up."

"By myself?"

"Yes."

"And where will you be?"

"I'm taking a nap."

Patricia did everything exactly as her mother asked and even added a little something extra; hammer and nails were in her backpack. Then she got on her bicycle and headed out. Jack had absolute confidence in his wife but needed distraction and went puttering in his workshop seeking anything that had to get done. Max and Sunday March were on the living room floor hunched over the stock quotations, initially the New York Stock Exchange, saving the NASDAC for technology dessert but reserving the OTC should they feel compelled to gamble, if they could get away with it. Everything seemed almost normal, but, of course, it wasn't.

Patricia was scared stiff pedaling away, getting angrier by the minute that she let her mother get her into this. Jack stayed in his workshop for three minutes and then slouched down outside their bedroom door, just in case, and Sunday March couldn't get Max to focus on making picks. Sunday March couldn't figure out what was going on. The rest of the family was like pieces of a time bomb about to go off and the clock was ticking. He was walking on eggshells.

The two detectives were on the car radio with Pasquale when they reported that Patricia had just pedaled past their unmarked car. "Follow the girl," he told them. "Call it a hunch. Just do it. I don't think she'll care." Pasquale was wrong about that. She did care. When she saw them slowly cruising behind her she was relieved.

Jack lasted less than five minutes. He had no idea what was going on with his wife but figured it would be easier to get it out of Patricia. "C'mon," he said to the boys. "Let's see what your sister is up to." His slightly guilty conscience forced him to peek in on Susan to tell her they were headed to the park but she seemed so peaceful he didn't have the heart to disturb her.

Susan Stanich managed to get everyone out of the house. Everything was going exactly as she hoped so she took advantage of the opportunity and was actually napping. She must've been dreaming because in her dream everyone was going in the wrong direction. Perfect.

For the moment she was sound asleep, waiting on George Adamson.

Chapter 14

He had no idea how Patricia figured him out but the girl made a fool of him. Outside of immediate needs his thought processes didn't run deep enough for that reality check. But she had played him at the mall, ridiculing, taunting. And he knew it. George Adamson, more enraged than ever, wasn't headed to Whatcom Falls Park.

The accumulation of insanity stuff that had been gathering now exploded and was loosed upon the world, headed to the Stanich household. His mind became a barrage of indistinguishable noise where neither thoughts nor words could separate out or penetrate in, just noise, a wall of bursting internal stimuli with no place to land. He was gone.

The rejection by his parents had crippled Adamson and then morphed into an overwhelming fear of them. He was unable to confront his abusers; few ever are. The anger and hurt their indifference bestowed upon him had no appropriate outlet, which is why it was unleashed upon unsuspecting strangers. He didn't fear them because they didn't know him, couldn't reject him. But he could hurt them for what his parents had done. That's the way it worked. That's the way it always works, the cycle of abuse. The object for retribution is invariably misplaced in time and place. That simple sequence alone nicely explains most acts of violence and virtually all war, and the origin of death addicts. Unfortunately, without the touch of grace upon his spirit Adamson would remain broken, his pain the excuse to justify harming others.

Now, because of what his parents had done, he would hurt Witch Woman beyond anything she could possibly imagine but he wouldn't touch a hair on her head. Instead he would kill everything the girl loves and she would know it was because of what she did. It would be her fault. Tick, tick, tick.

The damaged are often too self-absorbed for true introspection. Maybe it's a blessing that they remain ignorant of the source of their pain. It may be too deep to stir without breaking the container. Susan Stanich didn't want to add to Adamson's burden, just stop him. She viewed him as a person stuck in a bad infancy yet she saw no other way to prevent him from doing more harm. Left on his own, killing was the only way for him to achieve a moment of calm though peace would remain perpetually beyond his reach.

Susan Stanich was leery of rehabilitative efforts during incarceration. As she saw it, therapy within the penal system suffered its own self-fulfilling prophecy and killers had been let loose to prove the worth of the effort with disastrous consequence. She wouldn't take a chance on that happening with Adamson. Her intent was to insure there would never be any doubt as to his insanity; there would be no possibility that he could ever be released.

There are vibrations in the ether that the human mind is incapable of sensing, yet there is a sound argument that the ability to perceive such is within the experience of other creatures in the animal kingdom. For them there is more than that which five senses convey. As such, animals may be more aware than humans. In spite of our lording over the earth, filled with hubris, we stand further down the rungs of the ladder when it comes to evolution. Not so with Susan Stanich.

She may be a mutant, perhaps more animal than human. What insights and tools she has at her disposal enable her to scare the shit out of people like George Adamson, and then bend them to her bidding. For the most part, it will all be in their mind. That's where she goes, just as she says, unless some action more of a physical nature seems to be what's needed.

The energy in the universe is in a constant state of overlapping ripples circling out like raindrops in a pond, connecting each wave to all others. Grind it all down and everything is made from the same stuff and it's all good and it's all connected. If we survive the barbaric legacy from our predecessors long enough to allow our brains to develop, we will one day be capable of feeling the nudge of molecules from ripples light years away. We just don't know it. But Susan Stanich knows.

That day the forces about tied their energies together, she and George Adamson. Susan woke from her nap feeling his pounding heartbeat as he made the turn from the county asphalt on to the gravel road that leads to the Stanich residence. She was bathed in the poor man's madness, sadness, and desperation to find release from his pain. He would do anything for that reprieve and all he could think of that day to find relief was to kill as many members of Patricia's family as possible. Only in that instant, on the cusp of committing the deed would Adamson's peaking agony burst like a festering infection and give him a pause of relative painlessness. But Susan's compassion did not extend to allow him any window of opportunity to express that relief. Her intent was to add to his burden, layer upon layer. Just the same she knew his pain. As the young hooker on the streets of New York she had been him, trading humiliation at the hands of men for the shame at having been used by her own father. She knew Adamson's worthlessness and madness. Nevertheless, after that day he would never be the same and not for the better; too bad, but necessary.

Adamson parked down the road from the Stanich house as though that would provide cover for his approach. He's like a child Susan thought as she watched him from the kitchen window while she finished drying the last of the morning dishes the kids left. Usually Susan would do something fitting to remind them to never leave dirty dishes but she had excused the whole crew that day with the various ploys that had been necessary to get each out of the house. Poor, poor man she thought as she placed the dish towel back on the rack.

Adamson knocked on the front door; that direct, that simple, with the intention of slaughtering whoever answered.

Susan Stanich may be a witch but she's also a woman and wanted to look her best. After all it wasn't every day that she would catch a madman in the midst of a killing spree. She wasn't sure if Adamson would try to break in through a window or maybe open the garage door and sneak in through the entrance leading into the house. So, when she heard the knock she felt she had an extra half minute and took full advantage of the time to fix her hair a bit and quickly throw some toothpaste on her brush and give her teeth a quick round and round. Then she walked over to the door just as he was knocking for the second time and, with a great big smile, opened the door.

"You must be the killer everyone's looking for," said Susan. "I thought you'd be taller." After a pause to let things sink in, she added, "Who were you expecting George?" Adamson's insanity was stopped dead in its tracks. It didn't know where to go. Every conceivable possibility had crossed George's mad mind except something like this. Susan turned her back on him and stepped further into her house. "C'mon in, George, let's talk."

He followed her and at the same time slipped his hand inside his pocket and withdrew the knife he had used on his previous victims. A noise behind made him turn and look. As he watched, the front door closed by itself and the key in the lock turned. A horror he had never experienced began to creep into his being.

"Please put the knife away George. Better yet, place it on the floor or I might be tempted to use it on you." That he wouldn't do and instead George Adamson began to circle Susan Stanich. "I really wish you wouldn't do this," she said. But it was too late. The streetwise prostitute emerged and the witch Knife went into a crouch like a tigress about to pounce, her barber's razor was out in the same instant and she lunged. There was no cinematic circling dance or parrying of crisscrossing blades, no feints, nothing, just one blurring leap. And in that split second she cut the hand that held the knife just enough. He never saw it happen. As far as he knew she never moved from the spot where she was standing. In the same moment he felt a pain in his hand and the knife dropped to the floor. Only then did he see the bloodied razor appear in her hand. Her aggression penetrated his insanity and piled on more crazy. Then she cut his other hand to make sure he would use neither.

"Sit down," said a voice from behind Adamson. He slowly turned his head and found himself looking into the blue-blue eyes of a second Susan Stanich. He then turned back and found the first Susan still there. A piece of whatever was left of his sanity dropped out of his brain. From a third direction to his left another voice came: "George, sit down like she said. Just do it." Filled with horror without end Adamson peeked at the new Susan and collapsed on the floor where he was. A fourth Susan appeared on his right. Adamson began crying, clawing at the face that was now buried in his bleeding hands. His mind was completely gone. Soon catatonia would be all that was left. What he would never see were the compassionate tears that rolled down the faces of the four Susan Stanichs.

"George, no more," the four said. "No more," they repeated. Then like bubbles from a child's toy three of the Susans popped and were gone. "You poor baby," said the remaining Susan, "so helpless, so deadly." He didn't hear her. Like Eloise DeMarco, the woman who had kidnapped her daughter years before, he would never hear anything other than the noise in his head ever again. When the witch Knife is finished with a killer there's very little left.

He sat on the floor before her like a helpless baby. Susan tended to his hands applying enough pressure to stop the bleeding, then taping a gauze patch to each hand until he could be properly treated by a doctor. Then she called Lou Pasquale and suggested he come to her house when he could. Next she turned on the hot water for a shower while she had the time before Jack and the kids returned home.

George Adamson stayed there rocking back and forth, cradling his wounded hands in his lap. He no longer had any contact with the outside world, nor ever would. Only one thing penetrated his madness. His terrified eyes never left Susan Stanich when she was within sight.

Lou Pasquale and Stanley Millman were the first to arrive. Susan left the front door open, anticipating their arrival. Lou rang the bell anyway. Entering a house on the job without a warrant can be prosecuted as an offense unless there's an apparent felony or the like taking place.

"Door's open. C'mon in," yelled Susan from somewhere in the house. "He's on the floor in the living room. Take a look. I have his knife and the DNA evidence you might need if he's the one who slashed those girls. There could be traces of their blood. Maybe it's him."

The two stepped into the house and turned to their left. There on the floor was the pink Adamson holding himself, rocking. Lou knelt down in front of him and tried to get his attention. George Adamson looked through Pasquale as though he weren't there. Millman tried, adding a few words to encourage a reaction. Nothing. Then Susan walked into the room and the maniac began trembling uncontrollably from head to toe.

"This madman came into my house and threatened me with this knife." Susan handed a plastic bag with the knife inside to Millman.

"Did he break in," said Pasquale.

"Oh, no," said Susan. "He rang the bell and I invited him in. He seemed like a decent fellow. The last thing one might expect from a gentle looking soul like him would be a maniac ready to kill you, dontcha think?"

"Why did you let him in?" asked Millman.

"He rang my bell," said Susan. "He obviously wanted to come in. How could I know he wanted to hurt me? You tell me."

"How did you get the knife from him?" asked Pasquale.

"I got lucky and he dropped it."

"Yeah, and how did he get those nasty cuts on his hands?" said Millman.

"Self-inflicted wounds maybe? He is a nut. What do you think? Why don't you ask him?" They tried. Unfortunately George Adamson would never say another word as long as he lived.

"We're going to have a lot of questions for you," said Pasquale.

"Ask away."

"You can't go around doing these things," he said.

"Doing what?" said Susan. "Unless I'm mistaken a pathetic, insane man with an uncontrollable compulsion to kill is now in your custody where he can do no more harm. Do I have it right so far? Now you're making threatening noises against me. What are you accusing me of, catching a killer? Lou, you have to take a good look at your priorities. No more dead girls. What more do you need to know?" Pasquale looked at Susan. She shrugged her shoulders at him.

The two detectives gently picked up George Adamson and walked him out of the house, at which point Jack and the kids drove up. Patricia's bicycle was tucked in the back of the SUV.

Susan headed off any conversation by collaring her daughter with a shut-up look that Patricia understood when she saw the killer being led away. She shut-up. Lou

Pasquale watched the silent interchange between mother and daughter and wondered if it would do any good to get the daughter alone. He knew it was his duty to follow the hunch or lead yet in his heart he already knew it would be fruitless. Pasquale and Millman set Adamson in the back seat. Then Pasquale turned to Susan, thinking about what he could say.

"I can guess what's on your mind. Doesn't take a psychic, which I am not in case you're wondering," she said. "That poor man won't be hurting anyone anymore. That's all you'll ever know, all you need to know. Let's put this one to rest, Lou. Whattaya say?"

"Just like that?" he said.

"Just like that."

"We'll see."

"That's good enough for me," said Susan. Pasquale stepped into the car and they drove off.

"Back so soon?" said Susan to the rest of the Stanichs and Sunday March.

"Max," said Jack.

"Max what now?" said Susan

"Max said we were all in the wrong place," said Patricia, not wanting to be left out of the conversation. "He said we should go back home and finish doing the dishes."

"Really," said Susan. "Max, didn't you know I was doing the dishes?"

"You hadn't started doing them yet when I said that."

"Little fuck," said Susan. Max smiled.

Sunday March watched the up and back like a ping pong game in which he hadn't the vaguest notion of the rules, nor any idea why they were even playing. The Stanichs were a mystery to him, both him and Jack, which proves time spent with Susan wouldn't clarify a thing.

Lou Pasquale and Stanley Millman were credited with the capture of a serial killer. Yeah, the residents of Washington State were able to breathe a little easier. Debriefings for the media mentioned the Stanich residence only in passing. In his own self interest Pasquale provided no further information regarding the tip they'd received from Susan Stanich. For one he liked being a hero, but more importantly he didn't want to encourage a psychiatric review by his superiors that would surely follow were he to say what he suspected aloud. Millman accompanied his stance with the strong silent thing. Besides, the high profile capture of Adamson would lead to juicier assignments for the duo. That bounty they wanted.

For the time, Susan Stanich's official involvement with the department was put on hiatus. Except for an afternoon visit to the Stanich house three days after Adamson's capture that would be the last the detectives would see of her for several months. Pasquale and Millman relegated Mrs. Stanich to the back of their minds, though not a day would pass that they wouldn't be reminded of her. Susan's mystical energy sticks.

An attorney for George Adamson's parents was sent to provide representation and sign off on the documents that would release the contents of his condo to the authorities. Ghastly souvenirs from his spree were found confirming his guilt.

Adamson was incapable of standing trial by reason of insanity. He was confined for life to an institution for the criminally insane. On the second night of incarceration the light in his cell went out. In the days that followed maintenance changed the bulbs many times until they concluded there was something wrong with the wiring.

They tried rewiring the cell. That didn't work either so they moved Adamson to a second cell, and eventually a third, but the dark seemed to follow him and maintenance just gave up. Day and night he remains in the dark, huddled in fear, terrified like a frightened child.

In the coming years only one person would ever visit Adamson. That would be on the anniversary of his capture. Regardless of where she lived or whatever else she may have been involved in, on that day she would be sure to be in Washington State to sign in the visitation register and be allowed to sit with him for an hour in a cell. He would be in a straight jacket and chained to a bar, all of which was unnecessary. Susan Stanich wouldn't have let him harm her regardless. She was there to comfort him, to let him know that in spite of his insanity he wasn't forgotten, he wasn't alone. She would stroke his cheek and talk to him like a mother to her son because all he had done, all he had suffered, it wasn't his fault and she wanted to let him know that but for the grace of God she could be him.

Chapter 15

At last we come to the return of Alice Summers' and the death-defying capture of the unmasked serial impregnator. In all truth it didn't happen quite like that. In fact it was the kidnapper, whose only name is Alan Marcus, who dragged Alice to the police station, not the other way around. He was ready to atone for his sins, pay the piper, face a jury of his peers, own up, man up...do anything to be free of her and no longer under her spell. From the day he kidnapped her he'd suffered miserably, unrequited love with no hope of salvation.

Though Alice had promised to visit him in jail, after mulling that over Alan decided that wouldn't be in his best interest. The reformed kidnapper figured he needed to start getting over her as soon as possible so that he could enjoy his middle age in the event they let him out by then, hopefully before the gap in years between a man and woman becomes too big a stretch for him to find a nice woman for his old age. Oddly enough or perhaps nature's way of insuring propagation, a reasonable difference in ages during the child bearing years works. It's perfectly acceptable for a 30-year-old woman to partner with a 42-year-old man, or in some cases vice versa. However, it would be nuts and illegal for 24-year-old to date a 12-year-old; same age difference. And it would be equally unlikely for a 69-year-old woman to get the hots for an 81-year-old geezer, unless of course there's money involved. Money cuts years off a man or woman's age when they're on the make. So, age differences stretch in the beginning and at the end, but we're all the same age in the middle. Timing is everything. Alan Marcus understood this even if he couldn't figure out why he screwed up his life. Alice had to go, the sooner the better. I know all this sounds ridiculous. Even writing about it makes me wince a bit, but that's how we are, ridiculous, even at our best. Why sugar coat it!

Alice walked into the police station like Cleopatra with Caesar in tow demanding an immediate audience with whoever was in charge. The desk sergeant told her to take a seat.

"I'm Alice Summers, the girl who was kidnapped. Everyone's looking for me."

"Well, now you're found," he said, "so take a seat."

A graffitti artist, two traffic ticket scofflaws and a real runaway were ahead of the kidnapper and kidnappee. They sat fidgeting and bickering for an hour before Stanley Millman came down from his office and rescued the desk sergeant and a gang leader that had just been brought in. Pasquale refused to get involved.

"Which one of you is the kidnapper?" Millman asked the pair, setting the tone for the seriousness with which police and the courts would thereafter take the impregnation spree.

Alan was taken into custody and faced a long list of charges. Kidnapping wasn't one of them because the girls insisted they went of their own accord and free will. But statutory rapes, contributing to the delinquency of minors, etc. were piled on. Each day of his hearings the females from his harem attended the proceedings to cheer him on. They had never seen his face before and were mesmerized, catty chatting amongst themselves as to which of the children most resembled their father.

Tabloids didn't have to fabricate a thing. They took down everything just as it occurred complete with photos of the mothers and children, and presto they had a front page story that met their high standard of unbelievablity. Alan pleaded guilty to everything. He would do anything to speed things along to get away from Alice because she insisted on being in court for each of his appearances even though she didn't have a baby. It was exposure for her and agony for him. Unfortunately for Alice the media took photos of all the girls but her. She even tried fainting twice. Photographers stepped over her to get a better angle on the other 'victims.' In spite of everything her career was back to ground zero. Even worse, the head of performing arts at her high school insisted that she audition for a bit part as a back-up singer in a chorus. She had to endure a terminal case of Alice who. God laughed.

Mrs. Marcus, Alan's mother, wasn't prosecuted because her mind wasn't quite right; we already knew that of course. The district attorney couldn't see a jury convicting the sweet old lady of anything. Nevertheless she spent as much time in court as her son, just not on the docket. She religiously attended each of Alan's hearings to spoil her grandchildren.

Naturally, the babies, toddlers and cute kids also drew Lou Pasquale, who stopped by each time they were in the courthouse to talk to the little ones and go through his routine of tricks sure to elicit giggles or, at the very least, smiles peeking out of the corners of their adorable little mouths. Sometimes he discussed politics with them. Janice Goldman encouraged this.

Speaking of Janice Goldman...three days after Alan Marcus's capture Pasquale and Goldman were enjoying a delicious institutional lunch in the hospital cafeteria. She was enjoying ketchup on pasta, Italian cuisine. Lou put the ketchup on a tortilla and dined on Mexican. Janice was coming to the end of a 48-hour stint. The first 12 hours were her regular shift and the balance required that she be on call. Nine months prior there must have been weeks of endless rain because babies were popping all over the place. She hadn't been home in days.

"Unless I'm in the middle off a difficult delivery I'm off in an hour. I want to meet this woman."

"You can't just barge into someone's life."

"She didn't have any trouble barging into ours."

"We barged into hers."

"Make it official business."

"Janice, sweetheart, you know I can't do that."

Two hours later, Goldman, Pasquale and Millman were pulling into the gravel road leading to the Stanich house. The drive over was Millman's introduction to Janice Goldman. She peppered Lou's partner on the way seeking embarrassing tidbits from Lou's past to be used as ammunition in the future. Alas, the blue wall of silence prevailed and Millman wasn't the touch she hoped he would be.

Susan Stanich came out to meet them, carrying a broomstick. Patricia, Max and Sunday March were on the porch rolling on the deck. Jack stood in the doorway delighted by his wife's sense of humor, which as everyone knows is the secret to success for a happy marriage such as theirs. Without silly to bookend serious, life would be stressful as well as boring. Funny works.

"Here I am," said Susan, extending herself to Janice for a warm introductory hug. Then she stepped back and said, "Congratulations."

"Not yet," said Janice. "I want that ring first before we make it official, a nice, fat old-fashioned diamond." Then she turned to Lou. "Who has a big mouth?"

"Don't look at me," said Pasquale.

"In that case congratulations on your engagement too," said the witch.

"What are you talking about," said Janice.

"You're pregnant."

"No, I'm not."

"Oh, yes you are, about three days worth. I felt the two of you just now."

"Janice Goldman, meet Susan Stanich," said Pasquale.

In a rare moment of being caught completely off guard Janice looked at Susan, then looked around and found she was encircled by Stanich amusement. "I don't suppose you know the sex," said Janice.

"It'll be a boy," said Max. And their smiles got wider.

"See, I told you," said Pasquale.

"See what? This doesn't mean a thing."

"In nine months you'll change your mind," said Pasquale.

"Don't listen to him. I never do," said Susan. "Come inside. Let's talk."

And so the women spent the afternoon getting to know one another outside the dominion of officialdom. There was absolutely nothing in Susan's non-threatening demeanor that gave Janice the slightest pause that Susan was anything other than a beautiful, intelligent spirit whom she could treasure as a friend. They chatted, they laughed, and they bashed men. Pasquale, a favorite target, never left Janice's side. He and Janice were still too new to step outside their shadows. Besides, much of the talk had to do with babies and Pasquale was always looking for tips on how to endear himself to them.

Max and Sunday March spent the afternoon pouring over stock quotes on the internet and then dove into the financials on the corporate web sites of those that seemed likely candidates that could one day yield board and tuition for three. Patricia sat near them, buried in a book about witches that had only recently caught her interest. Since before her teens she'd set her sights on a literary career, always with an eye towards fiction. Lately she was of a mind to change that to non-fiction, which seemed to offer a richer outlet for her imagination. Contrary to popular misconception, non-fiction is every bit as creative if one selects a subject steeped in mystique. She decided that one day she would become the world's preeminent author of a new non-fiction genre: real witches.

As he and Jack were strolling the grounds doing the bonding thing Millman happened to notice a collection of fly rods mounted on the garage wall.

"Ah, you fish. I fish," said Millman.

"Just got back from West Yellowstone," said Jack.

"Ah, grayling country."

"That was the idea."

"How about that. How many did you get?"

"Got some nice rainbows."

"We throw them back. The meadow stream up in Centennial Valley is full of grayling."

"That's where we were."

"And you didn't catch even one?"

Jack put on a game face for the rest of the afternoon. Macho crap. No male is immune.

It would be months before the Stanichs, Pasquale, Millman, and eventually nee Goldman would get together again, leaving time for the dust to settle on recent events. The future would join them practically as family, the debating team of Millman's children playing the cousins.

There remained one slight problem that seemed to doggedly follow the preceding events; stalking gamblers. Though Max's special talent was attributed to luck, myth or rumor by most folks, there were diehards who wouldn't give up, convinced the boy could make them rich. They cornered Max on his way to school, coming out of school, in stores and at ball fields. On a number of occasions, police ticketed loiterers at the entrance to the Stanich driveway. Regardless, the most stubborn of the lot just wouldn't go away, worse than bedbugs. Neither Susan nor Jack could think of a solution that would get rid of them other than sacrificing Max and putting him up for adoption. But clever Sunday March had the permanent answer.

"It's easy. They're losers, right? Give them what they want," he said. "Get it?" So Max gave the high rollers the tips they were begging for. And they lost, and kept losing. Max turned out to be a bad luck tipster who once ran a legendary streak of winners, and that was that.

Alan Marcus was assigned to a minimum security wing. The warden and prison management were certain he wouldn't test the privileges that came with a generous amount of freedom by attempting to escape. Besides, he liked prison life and the food wasn't half bad.

Unfortunately for Alan, established visiting hours were Friday through Monday. The only time he had peace was during visitation off hours, which didn't leave much. Even worse, to pour salt on the wound, inmates were allowed up to ten visitors at a time. Babies and toddlers didn't count.

There's daddy," said the young woman, still in her teens, pointing to Alan who was reluctantly shuffling into the visitor's chamber. That was followed up by a chorus of 'daddy,' 'daddy' babbled out by his children old enough to talk. Virtually every visiting day the mothers of his offspring, children in tow, came to visit along with some of the grandparents, often including Mrs. Marcus, Alan's mother. Making babies was great. He had a lot of fun with that. But Alan was no Lou Pasquale. He didn't have a thing for the little ones. They irritated him and he had no idea what to do with them. Four days every week there were five of them crawling, toddling and running all around his feet, up his back and hanging on his arms. His lap was a favorite hangout. Alan was miserable. But one day the situation will be even worse for him. The sad time would come when he will be released.

Epilogue

Two easy weeks passed and the crazy stuff that scrambled the Stanich household in a dozen different directions was fading. From the outside everything appeared ordinary and for the most part it was, from the outside.

Sunday March, still adjusting to his good fortune, had stopped stealing from the classmates in his new school. Susan had threatened to chop off his 'fucking fingers' if he didn't and that encouraged his self control to act in his own best interests. One day half a dozen cell phones were missing from the backpacks of as many students and the next day they appeared again though each had someone else's phone. Under Susan's caring eye he began to rely more on his free spirited, outgoing ways to win the respect and affection of others, working towards no longer needing 'things' that didn't belong to him to provide that comfort. That's kind of the way it works, isn't it? We substitute 'stuff' for the love that we're missing. Everyone knows that.

Explaining his unique name was tricky. It took a while but eventually pride began to replace awkward. When someone would ask the origin of Sunday March he told them the truth, which almost always resulted in the same reaction: "Wow, how cool is that?" Sunday's sweet nature never let him forget where he came from or those he left behind. He began sending a card or note to the kids still at The Riverview Children's Retreat with little stories about what was taking place in the Stanich house, which the orphans took as Sunday's imaginative mind at work. He would send an episode every week or so for years. He never forgot them. And he would always have plenty of material to write about, didn't have to make up a thing.

Jack invested in topographical maps of the Yellowstone River basin and all areas within 100 miles of the national park. He convinced himself that if he put in the work and studied the surrounding terrain he would be better prepared to catch his first grayling, in spite of the fact that he already knew where they were. That's like memorizing a house plan to help locate a key that you know is sitting on a dresser. Compassionate Max understood his father's reasoning and poured over the maps alongside him. Good kid.

Detective Lou Pasquale and Dr. Janice Goldman got married. Even though she was quite pregnant by then the pair honeymooned in the Tuscany area of Italy and continued doing what they were doing before they got married anyway. They even went sightseeing one day for a few hours. Things did reverse themselves just a bit. Pasquale was no longer obsessed with Susan Stanich. Janice was. She'd found a girlfriend.

Stanley Millman continued arguing with his children and picking up the pieces when his partner's hunches fell out of Pasquale's head.

Patricia devoted her space to observing her mother. All of us are little pieces of our parents, the way we dress, act, and talk. We are the accumulation of everything that preceded us. But it's virtually always unconscious. Not in Patricia's case. She wanted to be a witch and figured if she looked and acted the part maybe it would happen. Susan caught on somewhat when she noticed Patricia looking at her kind of funny, showing up wherever she was, and taking notes.

"What are you doing?"

"Writing a book."

"About what?"

"Witches, it'll be non-fiction."

"Really? Am I supposed to be your source material?"

"You are, aren't you?"

"What's the title?"

"Mom Wife Witch."

"Write it but no one will believe you."

And this was that.

So, all in all everything was on track with one exception. They had no idea what to do with Max. But that's another story.

Twenty-five year old Mary Dell wasn't a very secure woman. She had given birth to her daughter Amy when she herself was barely sixteen. In the following seven years she bounced around in shelters and, when she could afford to pay the reduced rents, Section 8 housing. Her child was a worry that she managed to feed, sometimes in food lines, and clothe, always in thrift stores. But she was incapable of giving Amy the acceptance and love that she herself had never experienced. Amy was her responsibility, a burden.

When Dustin Campbell showed up in Mary Dell's life she was smitten with good fortune she couldn't believe. He was a decent fellow, a mechanic, and responsible. And he loved Mary Dell. Dustin saw her essence under the damage and he liked what he saw. They married two weeks after they met. The desperate life Mary had led carried over into her marriage. She tried too hard to please him, always fearful a day might come when she would be out in the world on her own again. Dustin was patient. He didn't try to make Mary better or change her in any way. He just loved her and did what he was supposed to, and then some. He was wise in that. Dustin also had a daughter about the same age as Amy and that's where the problem lay. Fearful Mary blindly favored Dustin's daughter to cement her place.

There's nothing subtle when one is on the receiving end of the pain from favoritism. It's abusive and there is rarely recourse because the person inflicting the harm is invariably the only one capable of stopping it. Complaints are usually labeled as whining and more often than not serve to increase the injury. In the rarest of cases, intervention may foster awareness and result in behavioral modification. It's possible, but it would require something drastic.

Susan rolled over in her sleep, hooking onto Jack with her leg. She was dreaming of a lonely little girl in hand-me-down clothes crying herself to sleep each night. In her dream the child's name was Amy Dell. Susan dreamt she would change it to Cinderella.

# # #

Mystic

A *spiritual experience invariably passes through trauma and occurs in an altered state. The expansion of consciousness necessary to acquire the clarity associated with a spiritual experience may be the same portal that precedes death, in an instant granting freedom from a world confined to five senses, bestowing a deeper understanding of reality, embracing profound sanity at the moment of surrender.*

To communicate the transformation that occurs may be nearly impossible. The interpretation will likely be metaphysical and necessitate a leap beyond the limitations of words or concepts, requiring a suspension of what many believe to be truth. An awakening may be an event that can be grasped only through experience.

It is the mystic who has stepped over the other side and lived to come back. I know. I am become the mystic as we are all to become mystics. I have touched the wisdom within that valley of death. It is of intuition and infinite.

M*ystics are borne of troubled souls to share spiritual gifts and cleanse from humanity an inherited barbarism whose foundation rests where evolution begins, to serve as heralds for waves of enlightenment, to point out the lights that hasten the path for any who choose to see.*

We each return with a message.

Gentle, gentle evolution becomes the sweet breath of each newborn.

Their parents are the air they breathe.

—The Witch Knife—

About the Author

From Silicon Valley to Northern Virginia, Jay Buckner has been involved in technology marketing for more than two decades. In 2007 he served as the director for the first USAID sponsored agriculture fair in Herat, Afghanistan. In his spare time this native of Brooklyn has written a number of plays and received recognition in the one-act play contest of the Actor's Theater of Louisville. Several of his plays have enjoyed limited productions off-Broadway in New York as well as Hollywood. In other lives he was a National Park ranger and a lifeguard at Rockaway, Queens.

Jay now lives in the Blue Ridge Mountains of Virginia to be near his children.

Other books by Jay Buckner

The Witch
Welcome to Afghanistan
Funny, Laughy, Sexy
Scenes and Monologues for Actors

Connect with the Author

info@bucknercreative.com

4996070R00103

Made in the USA
San Bernardino, CA
26 November 2013